19.95

Y0-CBH-314

SPRING NIGHT

By the same author
The Ice Palace
The Seed
The Birds
The Bridges
The Boat in the Evening

TARJEI VESAAS

SPRING NIGHT

Translated from the Norwegian by
Kenneth G. Chapman

PETER OWEN
London and Chester Springs

Translated from the Norwegian
Varnatt

PETER OWEN PUBLISHERS
73 Kenway Road, London SW5 0RE

Peter Owen books are distributed in the USA by
Dufour Editions Inc., Chester Springs, PA 19425–0007

© 1964 Universitetsforlaget Oslo
First British Commonwealth edition 1972
This paperback edition 2004
English translation © 1972 Kenneth G. Chapman

All Rights Reserved.
No part of this publication may be reproduced
in any form or by any means without the prior
permission of the publishers.

ISBN 0 7206 1189 X

A catalogue record for this book is available from
the British Library

Printed and bound in Great Britain by
Bookmarque Ltd, Croydon, Surrey

1

THE WHOLE HOUSE felt different because both father and mother were away. They had left early that morning and taken their full weight with them. It was fine to have them, but just the same: he could breathe easier now and was alone. These were Olaf's thoughts as he entered the house. He called it being alone; he did not consider his sister Sissel, who was at that moment sitting in the living room, to be any pressure. On the contrary.

And now he could do as he pleased.

Just let me!

He stopped in the hall to call out in a voice that would shake the house:

Oh–ho; what I don't know!

And then right away again:

I know more than anyone thinks!

That's the way you shouted when you were fourteen years old and did as you pleased. But it never came to anything, he could not get it out. Even though he had full freedom to sing out so that Sissel heard. He stood there a while and let his silent cry sink into him and into the air around him. He felt the unspoken words running up and down his spine.

The air was almost hot. They were in the middle of a heat wave which had lasted four days. It was really only spring, but late spring, on the borderline to summer – so it was light all night long. Just at that moment it was the evening of a broiling hot day. Olaf had on only faded shorts and a pair of well-worn sneakers. His steps in the hall made no sound. He was on his way in to Sissel who was listening to a request program on the radio – he could hear the radio whining through the half-open door.

Olaf remained standing where he was. Sissel was not as much alone as he had thought: Tore had come to visit. Tore lived not far away and hung around Sissel, so it was nothing new. Now he was there again and both he and Sissel were sitting with their backs to the door so that they did not see Olaf. They were sitting in front of the radio. Tore was tall and had a rather thin, studious face. He had just come home on vacation and was eighteen years old. Sissel was also eighteen, as she sat there dressed in shorts like her brother and stretched two brown legs out across the floor. She lay lazily in the chair as if to say: that's what I'm like.

Olaf saw it well enough.

What was it Sissel was turned toward? It wasn't Tore. He was just allowed to sit there. She was sitting as if she were only lazy, but she was probably listening for footsteps. Olaf was certain that she was always listening for footsteps. Come come, steps in the hall! – that's the way she was sitting.

He made his own steps silent. Remained standing still. If he went in, Tore would be bothered and cross – and he really had no desire to go in, anyway, while Tore was there. Maybe Sissel would also be cross. You never knew with her.

I can just go, he thought, but did not go.

A green eye on the radio played coldly and distantly toward him. Like northern lights. Bewitching, although it was really no more than a helpless machine. Out of the loudspeaker came many different wishes.

Otherwise everything was still. Sissel and Tore did not speak. Nor was there any wind or other sound outside. The house contained only the hidden murmuring of having been deserted by grown-up, weighty people.

6

Now I'll call out to them: I know lots more than any one thinks! That'll make them jump.

He just stood there.

Or I can just go outside again. To my glade. I can go out and knock on the wall and talk with Gudrun.

He did none of these things. Just stood leaning against the stairs out in the hall and waited for something in the unknown and looked in at the two by the radio. Tore must have just come, for he asked casually:

'Any good requests?'

'Oh – ', answered Sissel without moving.

'No, they just request the same things over and over again.'

'That's because so many people listen,' replied Sissel.

They must have been thinking about other things as they sat there. Tore asked, while his eyes rested on her:

'Isn't it cold to sit like that?'

'What do you think?'

'Don't think anything. But I like it.'

'Well, be quiet now,' she said and let her leg swing. 'You came to listen to the radio, didn't you?'

'Yes,' replied Tore.

Olaf wanted most of all to leave now, he told himself. He did not want to stand there like that any longer spying on them. But if he moved they would notice it and then they would know that he had been listening. So I'd better just stand here, he decided and watched them a bit guiltily, for he was very fond of Sissel.

The request program growled on.

Sissel spoke again:

'Move your chair nearer so you can hear better.'

'It's just kids who believe – ' began Tore, but moved his chair close to Sissel just the same. Olaf noticed how quickly he did it. Just at that moment a child's request came out of the radio.

Sissel said nervously:

'Listen to this.'

'What?'

'That kid. His request. Now he's sitting with his head right up to the loudspeaker.'

They themselves sat like children before it. As if it were not long since they themselves had sat close to the radio during children's programs. They began playing at it. Olaf saw it take hold of them.

'Like this,' the one said.

'Yes, like this,' came the muffled reply.

They touched each other lightly and fumblingly with their smooth, strained brows in front of the radio and right before Olaf's eyes. Olaf saw it and knew it must be something strange and good. The smooth brows which met and were still. Strange just to see it. Like a murmuring deep down inside:

What will this become?

For it is a beginning.

Smooth brows –

His pulse quickened slightly. The two over in the chairs sat motionless, brow to brow. Out of the radio streamed a child's request like clear little bells, and ended.

And the other ended, too.

'Sissel?'

Tore called to her, questioningly.

She straightened up. Olaf was ready to run, but she did not move, and he grew quiet again, spellbound by this game that he knew would some day also be his own game.

Tore asked quietly:

'What, Sissel?'

'I didn't say anything,' answered Sissel. But in a different tone of voice than before. Something had shattered. What was it? Olaf could not understand that it was anything. He saw Tore reach over and touch Sissel. Her smooth, warm skin. He thought to himself that if I had done that I would have touched her as lightly as when a leaf floats down. Tore couldn't have touched her like that. At any rate, Sissel said:

'Don't.'

Tore did not remove his hand as if he had burned himself, but he did remove it. What was it that had shattered? – and for no reason?

'Sissel?'

'Listen to the radio,' she said.

'I didn't come to listen to the radio!'

'No; but now that you're here, you might as well listen,' Sissel replied.

It appeared that Tore had every right to be angry. He said sharply:

'Why did you send me that note? Maybe you're going back on that, too?'

She tossed her head.

'I won't be any plaything for you,' said Tore threateningly and Olaf felt the bottoms of his feet beginning to grow warm. He pressed himself deeper into the corner in the hall.

'Fool,' was all Sissel said.

'Oh?'

'Yes, you just read that someplace, that's just what they say in books.'

'Is that so. Now you just take it easy, Sissel. I have your note right here in my pocket,' said Tore toward her tempting neck.

'I'm taking it just as easy as I can,' said Sissel and Tore started so that Olaf could see it. Tore's hand floated down again.

'Leave me alone, I said.'

'Why?'

'*Why?*'

'Well, then I can just as well go,' said Tore. 'But can I just see your face first?'

'Haven't you gone yet?'

This gave Tore an opportunity to be as angry as he needed to be. He had every right to grasp her by her bare shoulders and turn her around:

'Oh, be civil!'

'Be civil, yourself!'

Olaf watched as they began struggling. But they looked happy as they fought. Muscles strained and swelled up. Soft strains and twists. Seeking toward each other. It was strange and fascinating for Olaf to watch. He once more forgot that he had no right to stand there. Look at them! – The radio was playing and joined in with a crowing aria. Then their mouths met, for just a hasty moment.

'Sissel.'

'Yes?'

Tore stammered out:

'No, nothing. I love you, Sissel.'

She started. Olaf started, too, back into his shadow.

'No,' she said. Not to Tore, just into thin air. 'No,' she said again. 'You mustn't. You can't.'

'What mustn't I?' Tore burst out wildly.

'I can't explain it. I don't know – '

'Well, I can see that I just don't understand women,' Tore said bitterly. Sissel answered quickly:

'Did you really think you did?'

'But you asked me to come.'

'Not at all. You just read into it what you wanted to read in it,' said Sissel.

Olaf could see Sissel from the side. He saw how she pursed her mouth and said that. Tore was really angry now:

'Maybe you think there aren't plenty of others I could have?'

'Other what?'

'Other girls, of course.'

'Oh, no. Not at all!' said Sissel. 'What could ever have given me that idea? Oh, no,' she repeated.

Tore looked shocked. He stared at her pursed and teasing lips and jumped up.

'What's the matter with you, anyway?'

He received no answer and turned with a jerk to the door. Olaf saw it in time and ran out silently in his sneakers. As he ran, he heard Sissel shout out:

'Don't forget to slam the door, Tore.'

'I'll be glad to oblige!'

The door slammed loudly – far in back of Olaf who had managed to get in hiding behind some bushes near the porch. Through the bushes he saw how Tore walked quickly down the hill toward the road.

2

As soon as Tore was gone Olaf stepped out into the yard. But he did not go in to Sissel. He was upset and felt a dry burning in his throat. Sissel is probably sitting in there now sulking. He just couldn't go in to her.

Out of habit he stopped beside the yellow wall of the house. Looked up – maybe Gudrun in his world of make-believe would appear again.

The house stood alone above the road. It was not part of a farm, just a house with a garden and a little grassy hill around it. In back of the house the hill sloped gently down toward the woods – the house sat neatly on top. It was surrounded by friendly hardwood forest. On the other side of a small hollow rose the mountain. It was the last house the road passed before it started out across the wide, deserted heath – or the first house for those coming from the other direction. But it was not far to other houses: just beyond the woods was a large town.

The walls had been painted yellow long ago, but the color had flaked off here and there and, since it had not been renewed, scattered shimmers of silver had appeared. Olaf went over to the house and rapped on the wall with his knuckles.

He knew that it was just nonsense about this imaginary Gudrun and he never would have done it if anyone were watching – but he knocked softly on the wall and looked up at the small attic window and said to himself:

'Are you there, Gudrun?'

It worked – the answer came floating down from somewhere up there and sounded gay and eager:

'Sure – '

'Peek down, then, or I can't tell if you're just the same, Gudrun.'

Yes, the familiar lock of hair came to the window. Her eyes were shining beneath it.

'Are you going to come up and say goodnight to me?'

That was just like her – he expected her to be nice like that. Too bad he couldn't take it literally. It was only something good formed in her mouth. All the time she was talking she had the lock of hair and her brow and eyes over the edge of the window and she did not resemble any other girl he knew of. And the way she was so interested in everything that concerned him, even if it was something annoying! Like now: all he had to say was:

'Tore – '

A short, cold laugh came down. That was good.

'Do *you* like Tore?' he asked, sure of himself.

'Tore? No!' she answered.

'Really? Don't you like Tore the least bit either?' he said and felt relieved.

'No, he's nothing,' the answer came down. 'I think he's just a big bag of wind.'

Olaf felt better and better. But Tore could be still more thoroughly taken care of.

'And you know what he's got, Gudrun?'

'No, what?'

'A green radio eye in the back of his neck! – But he doesn't see anything with it.'

Gudrun laughed so that she could hardly stop and squinted until her eyes were only narrow slits – just as Sissel did when she laughed.

Then she went away. There was no more use for her for a while.

3

OLAF WAS CALM NOW. He stood sniffing the air. It smelled of rain. There was no rain in sight now, but earlier in the day there had been a couple of warm showers and a few claps of thunder – without it helping any. And there was clearly more rain coming. It was still, the clouds were flying low and it was just as hot. It was still good to be lightly clad.

It was a perfect evening to go down to the glade and look and smell.

His own glade.

He was on his way immediately. As so often. He had lived many of his finest hours there.

Down by the road he met Tore. Tore must have stopped. Was he thinking of going up to Sissel again already?

Olaf stopped unwillingly, a bit embarrassed, for it had been so real and natural for him to make fun of Tore and give him a green radio eye in the back of his neck.

'What are you doing here?' asked Tore. It did not occur to him that it might sound a bit strange.

'I live here,' answered Olaf as if he were talking to a stranger. 'Something wrong with Sissel?' he asked a bit maliciously.

Tore looked worried and angry.

'Sissel can take care of herself,' he replied brusquely. 'You don't have to get nosy.'

'Why don't you go home, then?' asked Olaf.

'It's none of your business, I said. Why do you have to go sneaking around bothering people, anyway?'

Olaf was well aware of his reason, but it was not the sort of thing you went and told.

'Come on down to the glade with me,' he said suddenly.

'What's there to do there?'

'Oh – lots of things.'

'I don't think there's anything for *me* to do there,' replied Tore.

A big bag of wind, Gudrun had said. It sure fitted!

'Well, all right, then – but don't go thinking that Sissel likes you any,' shouted Olaf with more courage than he really had. It was just something to throw in Tore's face.

He was sorry for it, too, for Tore answered unexpectedly, seriously: 'Sure she does, Olaf.'

'Just because she – ' Olaf began, but stopped. He could not give away that he had been standing there spying on them. He turned and walked away. Was Tore just going to hang around in the bushes here? Well, let him.

The evening deepened, but in small and almost imperceptible ways. On the borderline between spring and summer. It would be a warm night, free of darkness.

It was known as the wet glade.

Olaf had stopped in the middle of it.

The glade lay on the side of the mountain, but a vein of wetness ran through the steep slope. It kept the earth raw and dark, and certain types of plants grew there in wild profusion. The luxuriant growth made it smell different than other parts of the forest. Grass and trees, and the grass was full of bits of rock from forgotten slides. At the top was an overhanging ledge of rotten stone. In the open patches between the trees grew patches of angelica – and it was these large flowers more than anything else that had drawn Olaf to this spot so often throughout his boyhood. He would not have been able to explain what there was between him and them, but for him they were wonderful plants as they stood bristling grotesquely with their bursting wheels of blossoms.

There was no running water to be seen, but the rocks in the glade were almost always wet. The wetness seeped and oozed right out of the earth and the shadows.

And the snake was there.

No one had seen the snake for many years. But someone had seen it once, and it had never been killed.

The snake was the most alluring and frightening thing in the glade. Olaf had surrounded it with new thoughts each year as he grew older.

The snake was constantly in his thoughts when he was in the glade. Beneath his usual thoughts lurked something dark and ice cold. It could occur to him that the rocks were wet because the snake had licked them. At night it lay there licking.

Perhaps it would never appear any more, just lie in the many hiding places in the glade and look around from the tiny holes it peered out of.

If only one could help thinking about it.

But Olaf thought:

Maybe the snake is watching me *now* –

What if it is? He did not move. Stood still and erect. When he finally moved it was with quiet and careful steps. Then he stood still again. His ankles and legs were bare.

Maybe the snake is watching me.

Watching and watching.

The slope was covered by a whole forest of angelica. It was half turned from the sun, but the plants thrived in the slanting evening sun and the raw earth. Although it was yet early in the summer, the angelica had already begun to assume its stately form, rigidly lovely in its burst of life. It was all Olaf's, it was he who had shaken the seed out and then trodden it into the earth. Two years ago. Those from last year were now only a pair of large, veiny leaves.

The snake has been lying and watching while it all has grown, while it all has withered again. It's seen me, too, uncountable times. But what do I know about it?

Oh-ho! all that I know, he thought and let one thing glide along after the other. There was a faint sting in his heart from the rest: from all that he did *not* know, but only felt the effect of.

What was it now?

Nothing.

He sat down on a stone. The glade lay still as a tomb in the over-clouded evening. The multitude of herbs breathed quietly in the evening air, filling it with their fragrance.

Far down below, on the road, cars passed occasionally, but their passengers did not see Olaf. He sat high up among the bushes and trees, and the sound of the automobiles faded away among the turns of the road. The cars drove through a fragant sea and perhaps never noticed it.

I wonder if the snake is watching me? he thought.

His skin prickled at the thought. I think it's watching me from a tiny hole. Just watching.

A while later he said to himself:

It must be watching me.

Immediately he was positive:

It *is* watching me –

It could happen so quickly. Grow to certainty. The snake lay somewhere under a leaf. No sooner had the picture taken form than the pulling began.

I'd better go home!

He did not mean it, he did not want to go home, he wanted to feel that pulling, he wanted more and more to feel the strange spell that he thought had been cast on him from a hidden spot somewhere under a leaf.

Try to get up and turn your back to it, he said to himself and shuddered.

Was it all just something he imagined? He had already begun to doubt. But it made no difference – he was spellbound and it was not an evil spell. Then something began to vibrate. Soundlessly. But still, it was a vibrating and a ringing and a magic song. In his glade.

It became still stranger. He saw the angelica begin to whirl so that the screens of blossoms crackled – and he was immediately sure where the snake lay hidden. Up there! Right there! He could not take his eyes off the spot. A few tufts of grass. The snake was in there, and he had to go up there –

He shook with both fear and joy, caught up in it.

Up! Now!

He rose slowly from the stone. Walked forward with short, unsteady steps. You're just playing! he tried to tell himself. No, no; I'm not playing! He stared at the tufts of grass. It was delicious – and the angelica shades whirled like wheels, like dancing gowns.

He moved nearer.

My eyes are beginning to burn, he told himself.

Immediately his eyes began to burn. Smarted. It would be soon now. His eyes felt hotter and more intense – as if they could easily destroy and consume anything they rested on. He was right on top of the tuft and was about to step into it – No! The spell broke and fell apart.

Was something moving in the grass? He longed for there to be. A couple of blades of grass quivered and then were still again, or so it seemed to him. All was gone. The shades whirled no longer. Nothing sang or vibrated. Nor was anything delicious, he felt slack and empty. He found he was covered by a cold sweat.

He stamped on the ground and shook himself a bit. No one had been watching. And he could not tell about something like this to anyone. Not even to Sissel.

Oh-ho, all that I –

About Sissel, too – he thought and tried to lead his thoughts onto a new path.

Bright green grass shone in the hollow below the slope. A fine little field, with small clumps and groves of birches here and there. There would be large black snails down there this evening, drawn by the smell of rain.

The calm air was brewing rain. Angelica bristled in the glade. And what was hidden in tufts and under leaves? Strange to be surrounded by it all.

Olaf dropped something he was holding, crooked his fingers together behind his back and made soft, secret finger signs in his world of make-believe:

For angelica, snails, rain – he said silently.

He had to hurry home to Sissel who sat and wept.

4

BUT BEFORE he got that far, he stood face to face again with Tore. Tore had stepped out of a birch grove and demanded:

'What are you doing here?'

The same stupid question as before. Olaf could not bring himself to answer it.

'Are you going home to Sissel?' asked Tore again.

'Sure I am. So what?'

'You can say hello from me.'

Olaf had not exactly expected that, so he just nodded quickly that it would be done. Later he could have kicked himself for it.

'Are you going to hang around down here all evening, then,' he asked belligerently.

Tore just smiled happily and replied:

'Sure, maybe I will.'

'Do you think Sissel will like that?' asked Olaf impulsively.

'I'll stay here if I want to,' said Tore. 'No matter what you like, Olaf.'

'We don't want you hanging around here!' shouted Olaf back.

'Sissel does,' answered Tore and nodded in an irritating way. 'Tell her that I'm not far away if she wants to see me.'

Then he stepped lazily back into the trees.

Olaf meant to shout something at his disappearing back, but nothing came out. He went home.

Their parents had lived in the old yellow house ever since their marriage, so both Sissel and Olaf had been born there. Everything around was so familiar to Olaf that he usually hardly ever noticed it – but once in a while it flared up like a flash of lightning and showed how varied and wonderful it was.

Father was a teacher of mathematics in a large school over in the town that could not be seen from the house. The same school Sissel went to now. The quite large, but sorry pile of a house had been his inheritance and it was for this reason he had continued living there although it was far to the school and his work. Olaf had many times heard his parents talking about moving, but it never came to anything. Nor was the house ever remodeled, as was often discussed.

Vacation had begun just a couple of days before, but father and mother were not on any vacation trip – they had gone to the next town for the burial of father's brother who had died suddenly, and too soon, and they would be back already the next afternoon. Just the same, for a whole day he could do just exactly as he pleased. Shout in the hall – know that no adult eyes were watching.

Sissel was, as he had expected, not in an especially gay mood. When Olaf appeared, she was sitting in the good chair by the radio with her face turned toward the back of the chair and her brown legs tucked up under her. She looked up and he had been right: she had been crying. She was still lightly clad.

Naturally she was lying in a chair crying. He forgot Tore and all that business and asked her carefully:

'Sissel ?'

She started.

'Are you there again ?'

He shrank back a bit.

'What ?'

Her face became ugly and she said:

'You've been sneaking around spying. I saw you out in the hall when you ran out. Just sneaking around spying. Aren't you ashamed of yourself? Spying so you'll have something to tell mother when she comes home.'

He stared at her. What was she after? A fight? She blushed when she said that about telling mother. She knew very well that he never ran and told on her. He was shocked that she could be like that. He almost felt like hitting her. She said softly:

'Go away now, Olaf.'

'Why?'

He stood still.

'Are you mad?'

'I was when you stood there spying, I can tell you.'

He began to grin, for he remembered the sight of Tore, who had sat there a little while before and gotten a green magic eye on his neck.

But Sissel knew well enough how to handle him. Just as the cold, joyless laughter at Tore was about to come out he felt her arms around him. He looked into her eyes and lost all interest in spoiling anything for her.

'Olaf –'

'Yes?'

'Won't you be nice to me?'

He said nothing. Just wanted to be.

He received a secret little hug. Secret, although it was not at all necessary, they were alone. But it was worth more that way.

If he only had dared ask why she had been lying weeping in the chair.

'Tore's not crying any,' burst out of him instead.

'Fool,' she said and kicked the table leg with her thin canvas shoe.

He realized how foolish he himself had been. But it couldn't be taken back. He thought about Gudrun up in the window – she was always in a good mood and had a lock of hair over her eyes. That's the way it should be.

Another kick at the table leg.

'Did you hear what I said, Olaf?'

'Yes.'

They grew silent again, as in a vacuum. But such a vacuum should not be and Olaf burst in again – with the first thing that occurred to him:

'Come on down to the snails! They're out this evening. There's never been so many of them or such big ones as this year!'

He spoke loudly although she was just about as near as she could be. But he had hit it right. Sissel grabbed at it:

'Sure, why don't we – '

Then she looked into his face:

'But what's the matter anyway, Olaf? Won't you tell me?'

'No.'

'No. Well, then let's go down to your snails.'

Lightly and quietly they left the house.

5

WHAT ARE YOU THINKING ABOUT? he felt like asking as they walked down the hill in step. He could not bring himself to it. There was an atmosphere of vigor and color and longing – he heard it and felt it as a promise.

Lightly and quietly they walked, and were silent.

The green hill melted into the still greener little field between the birches. They took quiet steps because what they were going to was good.

Not a breath of wind. Olaf got a deep pleasure out of walking in step with Sissel. She was a good companion.

'We walk in step well,' he said finally.

'Do we?' she answered, deep in other thoughts.

Her legs were both longer and more beautiful than his, as she strode along in her shorts.

Here's where I last saw Tore, he was on the point of saying. Maybe Tore was still nearby. He said he would be. Is he behind a bush somewhere? That's all right, if he is.

Olaf said out loud, into the still evening, because there was no way to leave it unsaid:

'A green radio eye in the back of his neck – '

Sissel did not lose step, just asked:

'Is that a new invention of yours?'

He laughed to himself.

'Just a green eye in the back of the neck.'

She snorted. Asked no more about it. She was used to many such things from him. Just foolishness and nonsense.

Then they were in the little bright green field.

It was warm and yet half raw there. Just after rain and just before rain. The snails were out, just as expected.

They did not need to search for them, but rather had to step carefully in the soft grass so as not to harm those that were there. Here and there a longer blade reached up above the carpet of grass and stroked their ankles and legs.

'Look there – '

'Mmm.'

They lay down on the ground. The grass was cool and felt good against their skin. In front of them lay a couple of huge snails. Lay in quiet rest and stretched themselves out, coal black, apparently lifeless, but Sissel and Olaf knew that they were being scrutinized.

They did not say a word. There was no sound – with the exception of the lazy humming of a car somewhere on the road. A reminder that the ordinary world was not far away. But the snails lay glistening and black on a light green carpet and just existed. They were Olaf's snails, he had made an agreement with his father about it when he was four years old. For ten years he had had a feeling of ownership – it would be difficult to grow from it.

It was nice to be there with Sissel and watch them. He could very distinctly feel that he was lying there side by side with Sissel, who meant so much to him. Sometimes he planned dangerous things he would do if she asked him to.

He twisted around and got his hands behind his back to make one of his secret signs. A beautiful sign for Sissel.

Sissel whispered:

'Be still. What are you twisting and squirming for ?'

He laughed deep down inside.

'Lie still. You're scaring them,' she said again.

She whispered without meaning to. It came of itself: the snails were watching them.

Other things contributed to it, too. The silence was endless and the rain clouds were right overhead; the rain could have been shaken loose by a shout.

'Lie still yourself,' he whispered back happily.

She, too, lay there quiet and long in the grass – and had been given a couple of secret signs without knowing it.

His thoughts touched the unpleasant episode in the glade earlier in the evening and he was on the point of telling about it. For it was safe now. But he stopped himself. It was best not to talk about such things.

Still –

'Move now, snail,' she breathed.

'What ?'

'I was talking about the snails.'

The words were only lightly exhaled so that they would not do any harm, it was that still.

'They're lying there watching us – '

He recalled all the times he had hit her and kicked her. Bitten her. Pulled her hair so that it crackled. Told her off.

Well, she had deserved it every time, he decided, and was rid her.

'Olaf?'

He started. Had she read his thoughts?

'Yes, what is it?'

'Don't know.'

But when a question came like that, something valuable was already gone. He was amazed over how strange and incomprehensible a girl could be.

Maybe he should shout something out so loud that the rain drops would be shaken loose. The rain was hanging so loosely over his head that it was only waiting for something like a shout now.

'What's the matter? Out with it,' said Sissel.

'Me?' he said dully, despite his plan to shout.

She's nothing to be afraid of, he decided. Her face was right up to his. That face that he liked so much, with its slightly turned up nose and pursing lips. The lips moved. He watched them and needed to know what it was that he did not understand. He shouted so that it rang, because he became somehow afraid of her.

'*Tell* me what it is!'

Naturally she jumped.

It seemed that his shout rang just forcefully enough to loosen the raindrops. The first drop struck his brow at the same instant, large and tepid.

'Oh, Olaf!' she cried out in annoyance.

She was already on her feet. Picked at herself. Grass and twigs had drawn a meaningless pattern on her skin.

'Oh, Olaf.'

Olaf still sat in the grass, strangely happy and astonished. Had he loosened the rain?

Sissel picked bits of grass from her knees. The raindrops came down harder and heavier. It began to affect the snails, but just as a new pleasure, a small movement in something on one end – they had senses open for the heaven's rain.

Olaf said blankly:

'It's raining – '

'So I see.'

Was she angry? She was picking at her knee, a couple of soft drops of rain ran over it. The rain was so warm that it was good to feel it on a sunburned body – there was not the least need to seek shelter.

Suddenly he knew what he should do. He raised his head and shouted as loudly as he could:

'More rain!'

Simultaneously he smelled the wetness running down Sissel's warm back and shoulders. Don't be mad, Sissel, he whispered to himself.

'More rain!' he shouted.

'What in heaven's name! Be quiet!'

The rain hissed down.

'Look at it, Sissel!'

'Come on now, dopey, let's go home.'

'You don't know all that I can do,' he said and was on the point of giving himself away.

He felt how dangerous it was, how real it was, how strongly he felt his own hidden world around him – from Gudrun with her lock of hair up in the window, to the snails in the grass, to the glade and the staring eyes that bewitched him from beneath a leaf.

'Well, I'm going,' said Sissel into the slanting strips of rain. But she was not allowed to. Olaf was quick and grabbed her leg and held on tight.

'More rain!' he shouted ecstatically.

The rain increased. It poured down. He was a bit frightened. How could he possibly know that he did not really have the power to call forth rain?

Sissel's leg was good to hold onto, nor did she pull her foot away in order to go.

'Sit down,' he said.

She sat down.

They sat and let the warm shower of rain wash them, tousle them a bit, too, externally, but only externally: their hair, the small plastered-on garments, cheeks – internally they blossomed under it.

Blossomed; why? No way to know. No way to ask. They sat side by side and shared a thousand small memories. Sat motionless.

'So you can make rain, Olaf.'

He did not answer. Don't say such things, he wished. It was for him all too strange and solemn for that.

The air was filled with the hum of rain. He sat there bare and small, knew that he would have to give in and go home: it would soon be too cold, anyway. He heard the trees sighing and the earth sighing, saw the friendly snails grow shorter as the rain struck their backs. He smelled the gentle fragrance from Sissel and was happy to be a part of such a silent game.

Suddenly Sissel said:

'It's all your fault, Olaf.'

What? If she had said it as an accusation he would have been crushed – but it was said the other way, so that it rose up in him and made him glad.

It was nothing to answer. Nothing for Sissel to explain more exactly, either. Only some words to accept, and have, one strange evening when he found himself sitting in the rain.

They were brought to their senses by the pouring wetness, shivered and stood up.

'Now stop it,' said Sissel and shook herself and tried to laugh, without succeeding.

The rain would not be stopped, but stretched itself toward the ground like thin grey threads. The snails went unnoticed away. Olaf snatched Sissel's hand violently and they stormed up the hill as long as they could. Home to the wonderfully deserted house that would not have a single comment to make even though one were young and behaved as one most wished.

6

INSIDE THE HOUSE it was a bit dimmer than when they had left. Not from any darkness, but from the clouds and the rain. Olaf and Sissel had been warmed by their charge up the hill. They slipped into their rooms to rub and dry themselves. Came out again with light, fresh bodies and were dressed.

Thus it was in *their* world.

And now they would have a nice evening. No one had promised them that, it just hung in the air. They did not talk about it, just felt it in everything: the security and the freedom at the same time. All that had happened down in the field. The tempting odors. It was something to sit peacefully with – just the two of them in a tranquility.

Sissel was making supper in the kitchen. Olaf was wandering around a bit. Before they had begun to eat they were startled by an urgent knocking at the door, in the middle of the rush of rain.

What in the world?

Sissel called through the open kitchen door:

'Olaf, see what it is.'

Her voice was not very steady. Another knock was already sounding out there.

· Olaf ran out. Straight out into it.

It hit him hard, and nailed him fast at first – prepared as he was for something unpleasant by that threatening knocking. He saw a small group of people. Four of them. They had come up to the porch. Two men were supporting or carrying a young woman, and a young girl stumbled down the steps; it must have been she who had pounded so heavily and demandingly on the door. Now she was down with the others again and hid in back of them.

One of the men turned the burden over to the other alone, lurched

27

over to the post on the porch and pounded at it, meaninglessly and in confusion. He was a small tousled man with excited eyes and arms he could not hold still. What sort of people were they? The man waved his arms wildly in front of Olaf and shouted:

'Is there someone here who can help us? Who are you, anyway?'

'Olaf,' answered Olaf as he blinked and tried to get control over his eyes.

'But there are other people here, aren't there?' said the man and flapped a bit. They were now all on the porch out of the rain. The woman who was being carried moaned softly.

The other man, who was tall and young and had a dark, rigid face, cut through with a sharp question:

'Do you have a telephone?'

The fluttering man beside Olaf repeated it in a tiring, nagging voice:

'Have you got a telephone?'

Olaf answered numbly:

'We can't make calls now. It's too late – there's no operator on duty.'

This all happened with blinding speed, while his eyes were getting adjusted – only to have them staggered again when they fell on the young girl with a lock of hair over her brow. What in the world! – She was screened by menacing men.

'Sissel!' he shouted into the house.

The young woman, who was wrapped in a blanket, moaned. The fluttering man buzzed around:

'Telephone! Don't you have a telephone? What are you just standing there for? We've got to have a telephone. We need a midwife – My God! – and there's not even a telephone here! It's a matter of life and death!'

The young man cut him off:

'All right, now, just be a little quieter, Dad.'

The woman bit the edge of the blanket.

Now Olaf saw that there was an old car standing in the downpour far down the hill. These strangers must have come from that car.

'Sissel!' he shouted, as he stared at the well-known lock of hair which had suddenly appeared from nowhere.

Sissel came on the run.

The strangers were now standing crowded around the suffering woman. She was large and heavy, it had been a hard job to get her up the steep steps to the porch. They all turned to Sissel.

'Good evening,' said the fidgety man, 'you'll have to let us come in the house. She's just about to have a baby.'

Sissel started, and a strange look came over her face at his words.

Olaf looked at Sissel, and felt how wonderful it was to be swept along by this unexpected wave of events. He had recovered from the first shock, was now just excited. The way things could happen without the least warning on a rainy evening! The tall young girl stood looking at him. It occurred to him that she was about his own age. She had large, frightened eyes and had not made a sound yet. But was it possible that someone had such a lock of hair in reality?

Sissel opened the door wide and the woman in labor half walked and was half carried in. The fluttering, flapping man talked without pause about their trip:

'We came across the heath here and this came on us unexpectedly when we were right in the middle of it. So we drove all we could to get to a house – and this is the first one we could see from the road. But is it the first?'

'Yes, yes, it doesn't make any difference,' the young man cut in again. Don't waste time gabbing. We've got to get hold of a midwife. Is there one around here?'

'If you had driven just a little bit farther,' Sissel managed to get in, 'you would have come to a large town where they have a hospital and everything.'

'Sure, but that rotten car broke down here!' said the older man. 'Broke down, and there's no time to fool around with it. My God! – and there's someone else sitting down in the car, too – let us in now.'

He nagged and gestured wildly.

The woman who was being carried bit the edge of the blanket. The young man said loudly and clearly:

'We're inside now, Grete.'

He received no answer. They all disappeared into the house which had just a short time before prepared itself for a free and tempting evening of youth alone. Sissel lead the procession into her parents' bedroom. She opened the door and pointed in – she did no more, for there came a low cry of pain which seemed to cut to the bone. Sissel turned away and said that she would fetch some boiling water from the kitchen.

The bewildered older man came out of the room again immediately and asked Olaf where the telephone was. He had understood nothing.

'The exchange we're on is so small that there's no operator on night-duty,' Olaf explained again.

The man was already buzzing about something else:

'And there are more of us, too. There's a woman sitting down in the car, it's my wife, and she can't walk, either. We've got to fetch her. Nothing but carrying and carrying – '

Olaf wished that someone would ask the man to be quiet. The tall girl stayed close to him and sort of looked after him, but she said nothing about his chattering. She looked searchingly at Olaf and Olaf felt a kind of prickling on his skin.

She must have noticed Olaf's annoyance at the man, for now she stepped close and said very seriously:

'He really is nice.'

Her eyes were compelling.

'Karl!' shouted the man through the door to the bedroom, 'we've got to go down to the car and fetch Kristine. My God!' he said and dropped into a chair, apparently ready to let his voice run on. 'Oh, no,' he said resignedly, 'he won't come. So she'll just have to sit there. I've had a real shock, but I'll probably get over it soon – '

The girl went up to him.

'I'll go down, Dad.'

'You?'

'Yes, I'll go down.'

The fluttering man was quick, and took a firm grip on her arm.

'I've told you no. You mustn't be down there alone. Don't you remember how it was just a little while ago?'

'Let go,' said the girl, without result.

Olaf was not informed about the things they were talking about. But he could hear that they were father and daughter. He looked in suspense at the automobile he could barely see through the rain and mist down the hill.

'Don't go,' said the man with unthinkable weight and authority, and let go. Olaf thought the girl looked ashamed. The man stood up and began chattering at Sissel who came from the kitchen with water.

The girl stood in front of Olaf and explained about her father and defended him:

'That's just the way he is. And he really is nice. You don't have to be afraid of him.'

'Is he really your father?' popped out of Olaf. He was immediately sorry he had said it.

'Yes, why not?'

She looked him straight in the eye, held him fast in a way, so that he could not escape and think anything disparaging about her father.

'Oh, nothing,' he said quickly and thus took part in the acceptance of the unfortunate man she was lifting up. When she stood there that way there was only one thing to do.

'I liked him a lot,' he said.

'Sure. He's nice,' she said and her face shone.

With that they had each passed a test. The bewildered chatterer had been lifted up to the heavens and he himself knew nothing about it. They could now put him away as something they were for the time being finished with. They had become friends on a solid basis and in almost no time – for everything that had to do with the unexpected interruption of the evening's peace moved with dizzying speed.

Olaf asked eagerly:

'What's your name?'

'Gudrun,' she answered.

He jumped.

'You're kidding!'

'No. Why?'

'*Gudrun?*'

'Yes. I was named after my grandmother. What's so strange about that?'

'Never mind,' he answered, confused.

'Well, it's a common enough name – '

He said quickly:

'Oh, I think it's a real fine name. That's not why.'

'And you? You're name, I mean,' she said, a bit hurt.

'Olaf. Do you like it?' he asked, half afraid, and gazed in wonder at the lock of hair hanging down over her brow.

'It'll do,' she replied.

If he only could have told her how strange it all was for him. He trembled with joy.

7

OLAF WAS SOON GIVEN other things to think about: the stern young man, whose name was Karl, came running out into the hall. Actually, he had just barely been inside the room, he wasted no time. Had just managed to get the woman settled on the bed in there.

Now he headed straight for Olaf.

'We can't telephone from here and it's a ways down to the town, as I understand it. Your sister says I can borrow her bike. Can you get it for me right away? I don't dare waste time trying to fix that car.'

The older man butted in:

'But what about Kristine sitting down in the car? She can't just stay there – '

Karl became impatient and hard:

'She'll just have to, for the time being. You know very well what's most important at the moment.'

The man shrank back.

'Yes. I just don't understand any of this.'

Olaf was on his way to get the bicycle, but was stopped by a new sharp question from Karl:

'You have a bike, too, don't you?'

'Yes.'

'Then you can come along to show me the way, so that I don't waste time. Can't be helped if you get rained on.'

'Oh, no,' said Olaf, swept along by the speed.

'But how about her sitting in the car?' complained the man at his side. 'You've got to do something about her, Karl.'

'Yes, yes, yes,' said Karl and had no time for it. He turned commandingly toward Sissel:

'You can stay in there with my wife.'

Sissel stiffened. Did not answer.

'Aren't you going to? What are you doing just standing out here? Why don't you go in? It's not exactly easy for her, you know.'

He fastened his eyes on Sissel. She stood there flaming red. Olaf tried to look angrily at Karl, but Karl never noticed it.

Sissel stammered:

'I – I don't know if I – I've never before – I don't know anything about what I – I – I'm afraid.'

'Go in there!' said Karl like a sharp blow. 'This is no picnic for any of us.'

She looked at him. Then she turned and went in as he had commanded. She closed the door behind her.

'But she's sitting alone in the car and she'll be beside herself, Karl, completely beside her – '

Olaf heard no more, for Gudrun aimed right at him in order to wipe out what the man was blubbering about:

'Hey!' she said and ran her head into his side.

Olaf was a bit startled. But then he told himself that this was his

33

Gudrun from up in the window who had suddenly appeared – and it was just like her to behave like that. He accepted it as a means of getting away from the embarrassing spectacle of her father, for them both.

'Hey,' he answered softly and then there was no more. She was already off somewhere else.

'Come on,' said Karl.

'But she's alone in the car – ' they heard again.

Olaf got a shock when he looked at the man as he said that, he understood that all this about the woman in the car must be deeply troubling him. Something that Olaf as yet knew nothing about, but perhaps would become involved in soon enough. That's just the way it should be, he thought with satisfaction. This was really something! Hustle and bustle out of the ordinary. And the way Karl was – he just swept you along and showed no consideration. And this was all nothing to cry about. It was no tragedy. On the contrary, it would become something wonderful. The unpleasant feeling that had paralyzed him when he first saw them all standing on the porch had just been a passing blindness. A child was going to be born and that was always great.

Yes, when it's all over, he thought quickly. He could hear that it was not very great in there now. And Sissel was right in the middle of it –

He grabbed a raincoat from the wall and ran out into the wet evening with Karl.

They set off down the hill so that the bicycle wheels sang and popped and the tires hummed in the mud on the driveway. In no time at all they were down by the old, broken-down car. They had to slow down there.

Just beyond the windshield – and Olaf started. There was a searching face close behind the windshield. The glass was striped with raindrops, but he still could see the face shining clearly. Then he heard a loud knocking on the glass and the window was rolled down. The face came naked through the opening, terrified and hard at the same time, with fixed eyes.

34

She had managed to do it unbelievably quickly, as they passed on their bicycles in the sharp turn.

The woman made no sound. Sat there dumb. But Karl shouted: 'You'll have to wait!'

Then he was gone. Past the car and begun to ride down the driveway again. Olaf did not get away: a voice in the window said quickly as lightning and softly:

'Who are you?'

'I live in the house up there. Showing him the way – ' answered Olaf with the same speed.

'Will you help me?' said the voice in the window intensely.

'Yes,' he replied without hesitation.

'Remember that, now!'

'Yes.'

An impulsive promise, head over heels. Because her voice was like that.

'Hey! Come on!' shouted Karl from down on the road and Olaf shoved off and caught up to him.

'What were you doing up there?'

'Nothing.'

'Well, let's get going,' said Karl. They rode so that the wheels whined. Side by side. Olaf thought about the woman in the car. She was too young to be the mother of Karl and Gudrun. Their father must have gotten married again.

'Why is she sitting like that in the car?'

'She can't walk. Been like that a whole year. Dad has had to carry her a whole year now.'

That sounded strange.

'Today she stopped talking, too,' said Karl. He said it sort of unintentionally and mumbled something afterwards.

'What?' shouted Olaf.

'She can't talk any longer,' said Karl, angry that he had to say it again. They had to shout in order to make themselves heard in the rushing of the rain and the drumming on the raincoats.

Olaf could not bring himself to say that he had just heard her talk.

What would come of this? And what was it he had promised to help her with? He would find out. It was exciting. He was glad he had been asked to help. His bicycle sang and there was life and song even in the weather around him. They rode furiously, were only two coarse stripes across the fabric of rain. The road was deserted.

'How much farther is it?' asked Karl impatiently.

'Not far.'

'Can I go faster?' shouted Karl, although they were already pumping with all their might.

'Sure!' called back Olaf exultantly.

For it was in reality an exultant trip. They were the emissaries of a young woman who was going to have a baby and who would be made much of in the future. For her they rode like a blaze of lightning through wind and rain; it was a joyful trip. When it's all over, when it's all over – and we're helping to bring that about! The speed filled them with pride. The knowledge that the young woman was in difficulty while she was waiting for her great joy was transformed into stronger thrusts against the bicycle pedals, but it was not a sorrowful knowledge. The face of the man beside Olaf was strained, he was withdrawn and strangely somber, but now he obeyed the slightest indication of the way from Olaf. Through wind and rain. Getting wet meant nothing. All this applied to Olaf; he knew nothing of what was going on inside of Karl.

'What's your name?' shouted Karl.

'Olaf.'

'You must have heard my name already. Karl.'

'Is Gudrun your sister?'

'Gudrun is my sister. But we'll talk together later when we can hear better.'

'What?'

'Talk together. Later.'

Olaf could not look over at Karl, he had enough to do just steering the bicycle in such blinding weather and at such high speed. Talk together? Later? What did Karl mean? Had he said it in a special way? Nonsense.

It had not taken long, he thought. They had arrived.

'We can call from here. They're on a line with a night operator.'

Olaf hurried in, with Karl at his heels.

Inside the house they started things going with urgent calls. Sent for an experienced midwife. Then they were on the way out the door again. Oh-ho!! sounded deep down inside Olaf.

How suddenly everything had been changed. At home the whole house was turned on end and mother and father, who had left that afternoon, had not the faintest idea about it all. And something inside him wanted it just that way, and filled him with elation and made him pump the bicycle with more than his own strength. Down under it all he knew that it was Gudrun.

Karl shouted at his side:

'I see now that it wasn't very far.'

Was it now that they should talk together? Olaf waited, but Karl said no more, just looked stern. Now everything depended on whether the woman in the car let things go along so smoothly.

The car was standing there out of action and lifeless, washed bright by the rain. The windows appeared to be blind. But in back of them sat a woman with a sharp, nervous face.

Karl said cautioningly:

'We won't stop there now.'

Olaf did not dare ask why. But if she knocks on the window to me, I'll stop, he knew.

Let us past!

She guards the way.

Karl got past, he hurried up the hill to tell as quickly as possible the one in need that help was on the way.

Olaf heard a bone-hard knocking on the window and stopped.

8

HE FELT IT as a paralyzing drumming. He stopped immediately. Karl hurrying up the hill never looked back, and disappeared into the house.

The woman rolled down the window.

'There you are,' was all she said.

'Yes.'

'I kept an eye on you, so you couldn't sneak past.'

A strange face in the window. It immediately occurred to him that there was no joy here.

'What do you want me to do?' he asked quickly.

'Stand by me if I need you. You can see that I'm here like a prisoner.'

Can't she talk any longer? thought Olaf puzzled and looked timidly at her.

'I don't know what this is all about,' he said gropingly. 'It's really none of my business.'

'It is now,' she said stonily. 'Whether you understand it or not.'

The rain drummed on the car roof. The woman appeared to be annoyed by the sound, listened to it with an annoyed expression. Then she turned to Olaf:

'It's getting closer and closer around me. Do you think it's any fun to see the walls come creeping in from all sides?'

Olaf became frightened. He realized that the woman was not quite right.

'No, I guess not.'

'It's been getting closer and closer around me,' she said. 'Now I only have a little room left. Today the end came to talking, too.'

'What? Isn't this talking?' asked Olaf and forgot to be careful.

'Yes, with you,' she said. 'But it's just as close other places, just the same. I can see that you're afraid, but you stopped when I signaled for you – so it'll have to be us two who hold together. I'm going to need you. What's your name ?'

'Olaf.'

'All right, Olaf. Let's get a look at you – '

He stood there and held out. Those eyes peering out from between walls coming closer and closer. She looked like a dangerous bird in a safe cage. But no safer than that she could grab out and hold anyone who came too near. Olaf had been caught by her, he stood in the rain in front of the open car window. It was getting closer and closer around her, she had said, and it was as if there were a dangerous fire in there.

'Have they come safely under a roof ?' she asked unexpectedly.

'Yes, they're up in our house. The only one home now is my sister, but help is coming right away. And they'll probably be coming down here now,' he finished a bit suddenly.

She gave no answer to that, switched to something else :

'You don't know what happened in this car just before it stopped, do you ?'

'No.'

'So he won't be coming down to get me so soon. I'm talking about my husband. You must have heard him jabbering away up there.'

'There's nothing else he talks about, except coming down and getting you!' said Olaf quickly and was happy he could say it.

It must have been getting closer and closer inside the car, for she stretched her body and got her head out the window a ways, as if to get air.

'He just does that because he's afraid,' she said. 'He's scared to death now. He wishes things on me, and gets everything he wishes. You don't understand that, you're just a kid, but it helps me a bit to tell you. I'm being destroyed step by step, it's his doing. He wished I was dumb this evening. A little while before the car stopped.'

Olaf did not dare move. This woman must be sick.

'Come nearer,' she suggested. 'Come on in here and don't stand in the rain.'

He obeyed, opened the car door and crept in. He could smell the broken-down motor. Broken-down and dead. The dangerous pent-up bird drew itself together.

'It's not safe for it to be any closer around a person than it is around me now, Olaf. I'm not talking about the room *here*. Are you listening?'

'Yes, but he – '

'Tell me!'

'I know he really is nice! Somebody said so this evening,' said Olaf. 'Somebody up in the house.'

'Yes, Gudrun told you that, I can hear that. That doesn't mean a thing. She's not my daughter, she's just his.'

Olaf did not answer. The woman began again:

'No sooner had he said it, than my tongue stood still. He'd been almost nagging us to death on the road. And maybe I said something a bit harsh, too. And Karl's wife had moaned and carried on all the way across the heath. She thought she was going to die because we never came to a house. But it was me who was going to die a little more, that nice Hjalmar saw to that. Wasn't he nice? He wished I was dumb – and right away I was.'

'But it's not true!'

'Isn't it true? If someone stood over me with an axe, I still couldn't say a word if I knew it would reach his ears. It's that bad.'

A chill ran down Olaf's back, both from the dampness and from the words.

'We'll have a run-in before the night's over,' she continued, 'and then we'll see who can take it best. None of us can take it, for that matter, but – . He can either let me sit here or come and get me, it's all the same to me. Now you can go up and take a good look at him. Have you heard anything I've been saying?'

'Yes,' said Olaf, frightened.

'Would you go up and ask him to come and get me right away?'

'Yes, yes, but there's nothing else he wants to do, either. He just had to wait for Karl.'

He expected that would make her happy, or something, but she had shut herself in again. Did not hear it. Olaf got the door open and tumbled out. Now something really new was beginning.

He heard a horn in back of him, a car swung past the dead automobile and drove up the hill. Olaf ran after it.

9

THE CAR SWUNG to a stop beside the porch. Olaf watched as the midwife climbed out and was met by Karl. Karl quickly led her inside. Shortly after, Olaf also reached the porch and took his raincoat off. Naturally, the fluttering man came out just then.

'Is she going to have to sit down there all night?' he asked.

Olaf shook his head.

'Did you see her?'

'Yes. Is everything all right here?' asked Olaf to change the subject.

'Yes, it must be, now that help has come. But – '

'Is Sissel, my sister, in there?'

'No. Your sister did all she could,' said the man, 'but now the midwife has sent her out anyway. She shouldn't be in there.'

Gudrun came out of a door and Olaf felt a thrill run through him. It was unbelievable that she was really still there. She smiled to Olaf so that he could be sure of it.

'Did you get wet?' she asked.

'Ahh, no,' he replied.

'Gudrun, you have to get Karl out here!' said the man. 'Now he can – '

'Yes, Karl's coming now,' said Gudrun. 'He just had to explain a few things.'

'This is going to end bad,' said the man. 'You'd think Karl didn't know who it was sitting down there waiting.'

'Be a little quiet now, Dad.'

'I just don't want anything to happen here,' he said, 'but nobody listens to me.'

A sound came from the bedroom. All three of them started. The man mumbled:

'Oh, dear; oh, dear – '

Gudrun looked directly at Olaf and informed him, who was a boy:

'That's just the way it is.'

Karl came running out. Gudrun was standing near the door when he opened it. They were in the living room now. The door to the bedroom opened from there. Karl said sharply:

'Are you standing there eavesdropping? Get away!'

He had been upset by something inside the room. Gudrun blushed.

'No,' she said timidly.

'You can just stop standing there like that,' said Karl, paying no attention to her denial. He grasped her roughly by the arm and threw her aside. Then he quickly went out. His father never had a chance to get a word with him.

Olaf was boiling. What sort of a heel was Karl, anyway? To treat Gudrun like that.

Gudrun pulled at his arm and whispered:

'That's just his way. He's just all upset now. *Nobody was as nice as Karl was.* But he was in the war.'

Olaf did not know how to make sense out of all that. But it fitted in well with Karl's face, with what he had heard and thought about the war which had ended a few years before and in which many people had taken part.

'He was injured. He never talks about it, but – ' said Gudrun.

Her father was standing by the window looking out at Karl. Karl was getting something out of the midwife's car. Olaf would have no peace until he found out what had happened in the other car before it stopped. He had to ask:

'Did they say anything in the car?'

It sounded stupid.

'Say? What do you mean?'

'Karl told me a little about it.'

Gudrun looked timidly at him:

'I don't want to talk about it. Karl didn't, either.'

Karl came in again and went directly to the bedroom. No one could stop him.

'I'm coming!' he said as he hurried past.

Olaf chewed at the answer Gudrun had given him. He changed the subject and asked about her father:

'His name is Hjalmar?'

'Yes, Dad's name is Hjalmar. We call him "Butterfly," too, and other things. The woman in the car is named Kristine. She's nobody's mother. Dad remarried.'

'What does your Dad do?' he asked softly.

'Nothing now. He used to work in an office, but then he couldn't manage it any longer and was pensioned on account of his health. He just fluttered too much finally. But Karl was able to take over his job, so that was good. Now we're moving – and in that awful car, too – ' she ended.

Olaf saw how the lock of hair fell down over her brow. Just as always, he thought. Strange feelings streamed through him.

A sound from Grete in the bedroom stopped everything. And Sissel had been in there before! he thought. She who didn't dare go in in the first place. He had caught a glimpse of her, confused and frightened, but inspired. It was good she had been sent out. But where was she?

Karl came out again immediately as he had promised and turned to his nagging father:

'Now I can go down to the car with you, Dad, and fetch Kristine.'

The father jumped and said:

'Maybe it's too late – '

Karl's handsome, strained face darkened.

'We'll have no such talk,' he said sharply. 'But you're afraid to go down there, I know that. So I thought it would just be good for you to wait a little. So you could get your thoughts collected a bit.'

The father just fluttered and said 'My God' over and over again. Put his raincoat on.

'You come, too,' Karl said to Olaf. 'Maybe you have an umbrella to hold over us on the way up.'

Olaf obeyed like a machine. Once more out into the wet weather. They took with them in their ears a new cry of grief from the house. They knew that it would grow and grow still more, could not be stopped – there was something so terrifyingly merciless about it.

Karl and his father walked down the hill side by side. Olaf came close behind them and looked at their backs: the one straight, the other worn and weak. Olaf was ill at ease. But he had at any rate had his wish for excitement fulfilled.

'What are you thinking about?' asked the father nervously and aggressively.

Karl answered calmly:

'Not about your affairs, if that's what you're worrying about. I was just thinking about the kind of pain that towers sharply up and up and up until it breaks.'

The man started.

'Strange way to talk.'

'It's not so strange right now, is it? Grete and a sharply rising wall as in a tower of pain.'

The father said quickly and softly 'shhhh.' They had come too near to the car.

Closer and closer, she had said, she who sat trapped in there. The car now looked as if it housed no living soul – stood there black and old and dead, while the rain drummed on the roof.

But she was sure to be sitting in there waiting. Her husband flapped his arms a bit and said softly to Karl:

'This isn't going to be easy – '

Karl said:

'She's what you've made her.'

The father fluttered a bit.

They could not catch sight of the face behind the steamed-up window until they were right on top of the car. They were as prepared for it as they could be and took it calmly, but it was not a pleasant sight. The face appeared somehow to swell up in back of the window – and then faded, drew itself into the depths of the car and hid away.

Her husband opened the car door and put his head carefully inside.

'Kristine – '

It looked as if he had forgotten, and actually expected an answer from her.

No, then he remembered that she had become dumb and had to go along with it. First he looked at Karl with an expression of sudden need. Then he turned to the woman and said calmly and lightly:

'Everything's fine now with Grete. We've gotten her under a roof for the time being and the midwife has come. So Grete's in the best of hands and everything seems to be all right.'

Calmly and lightly, but he did not succeed in hiding how nervous he was. No answer came from inside the car.

'Kristine ?' he said.

No sound.

The man backed out of the car and shook his head.

'It's just the same now,' he told them. 'We'd better just take her and carry her up.'

'We can try to get the car started now and drive her up,' replied Karl.

'You can't get the car started fast enough for this,' the man said and flittered around. 'It'll soon be too late.'

'Hold the door open there,' he said to Olaf.

Karl looked as if he believed nothing of what his father said, but said no more about the car. Instead, he climbed halfway into the car and took a firm hold. The prisoner came out, with her helpless feet and her shining eyes. It was no emancipating light they shone with. Olaf was the first of them strafed by its beam and felt it go through him. Closer and closer was its message.

Her husband took hold of her with an accustomed grip as soon as

c   45 he could. They picked her up in a matter-of-fact way which told of much practice. Olaf looked at her and knew that she had recently been wished dumb, too. He must have regretted those words now, he who had said them. He just carried.

'Slam the door, Olaf,' he said, panting, 'and then hold the umbrella over here.'

Olaf held the old, broad umbrella over the woman – and they moved up the hill. They carried her calmly, but they were also on guard, as if they constantly expected her to do something. She sat on their arms. She did not attempt to say a single word. If Olaf had not talked with her earlier in the evening, he would have believed she really was dumb. He who had made her that way puffed heavily up the hill. Karl walked curtly and withdrawn into himself on the other side of the woman. Karl who had been in the war somewhere out in the world. It was not likely that any of the others had found out what *he* remembered.

The weak man puffed and carried in a way that was irritating when there was a stronger person also carrying: he struggled and lifted and tried to carry more than his share. Karl, who was young and strong, had only half a burden.

'Do you have to carry all by yourself?' he asked irritated.

The other was on the point of losing hold.

'No, no,' he answered quickly as if he had been caught at something shameful and wrong – and let the weight of the burden shift over to Karl. But just for an instant, then he groaned and bore it again. Karl was tall and took long steps. His father had trouble keeping up with him. He mumbled while he carried, in a forced, unnatural way:

'It'll work out. It'll work out. Sure it will.'

Who was he saying it to? It fell to earth because no one listened to it. His wife certainly did not appear to hear it. But for him it must have been a heavy promise, judging from his way of saying it.

When they reached the porch the older man was almost finished after the hill – they had to let their burden sink down onto the bench there. They were under a roof, anyway. The woman had not said anything. Gudrun was waiting on the porch and Olaf watched her closely to find out how she would take it.

Gudrun withdrew into a corner. Terrible things must have happened just before the car stopped. Olaf went over to her.

'Leave me alone,' she said.

'Are you afraid?'

Gudrun nodded.

The man carried the woman into the living room, and set her down in the good chair by the radio – where Sissel had recently sat and stretched out.

From the bedroom came disturbing sounds. The woman in the chair sat as if she noticed nothing while Olaf, Gudrun and the older man bumped into each other in their confusion without realizing it, under the influence of what they heard.

Karl stood rigidly in the middle of the room.

Olaf whispered:

'What's the matter with Karl?'

'That's just the way he is,' whispered Gudrun back and did not look as if she wanted to, or could, tell more.

A cry of need came from within the bedroom: a call for Karl. Gudrun and Olaf looked accusingly at Karl standing there weighed down by the struggle: after all, it was Karl who had made Grete that way. They bored sharp eyes into him. He did not notice it. But his father pointed and said with unexpected authority:

'Go in, Karl.'

Karl went, stiffly.

To those who were left in the room the man said:

'*That* will soon be over – '

10

GUDRUN GRABBED OLAF by the arm when Karl had left and pulled at him:

'It would be better for us to be somewhere else.'

But they still did not leave the room. Just went as far from the two by the radio as possible. It occurred to Olaf that these two were certainly not sitting there with their brows together.

Sissel peeked in from the kitchen. Then shut the door again.

The man fluttered around. Fussed with the radio a bit, threw the music from one wavelength to another, started, turned it off, moved the chair, whistled half a tune and caught himself and stopped. The woman in the chair sat as if he were air.

Gudrun said softly to Olaf:

'She's so sick of Dad that she's been really ill from it many times. Everybody gets sick of him because of his chattering, and say that they can't stand it.'

'You, too?'

'No.'

Olaf did not look at her; he felt somehow that she ought not to tell such things about her father. He asked quickly:

'Why can't she walk?'

'Mother was sick a year ago,' Gudrun answered brusquely. 'Yes, I call her mother. She hasn't stood on her feet since. Just says she can't – and Dad has to carry her every day.'

Olaf stared and Gudrun said quickly:

'We don't know anything about it.'

'No – ' said Olaf and looked away.

'But he really is nice,' Gudrun insisted stubbornly. 'He just carries and carries her.'

Olaf had to look at the two beside the radio again. They sat there as if they were playing some sort of mute game no one else knew. The man flitted around, chattered, picked things up and put them

48

down again. The woman sat motionless in the chair. Olaf was on her side and said:

'But I guess he wasn't so awfully nice in the car.'

Gudrun looked at him quickly:

'What do you know about that?'

'Just heard about it. That's the way it was, isn't it?'

'No one was nice in the car,' Gudrun replied curtly.

Sissel came out of the kitchen to go up to the attic. She did not look like she could be spoken to. Olaf made an attempt anyway when she came back.

'Out of the way,' was all she said.

Her hands were full.

'Oh, Olaf,' she said, softly and confidingly, so that it went right through him.

'Was it bad when you were in there?'

She nodded.

'If only mother had been home! Find out when that girl wants to get some sleep. It's late already – she can use your room, Olaf.'

'My room?'

'Yes, you can sleep in a chair. There aren't enough beds for everyone.'

Then Sissel ran out. If only mother had been home, she had said. Already. Olaf had had that secret wish for a long time, too. But who would have thought that everything would have been turned upside down that way just this evening?

He had felt it as a sort of sweet shock when Sissel had said that Gudrun could sleep in his room, his bed. He would be glad to sleep in a chair.

He turned to Gudrun and his cheeks were warm:

'Do you want to get some sleep, Gudrun?'

She did not understand right away.

'Sleep? Me? No. We're not going to bed, are we? Who could go to sleep when – '

'No,' he said. 'But when you get tired, you can go to bed, Sissel told me to tell you.'

'All right,' was all she answered.

The man by the radio had also heard and immediately butted in:

'Go to bed! Are you talking about going to bed? Do you want to go to bed?' he asked the dumb woman. 'The girl here in the house has promised that you can have a bed.'

He received no answer, no sign – and shrunk back.

She looked him calmly in the face. She had extinguished the glow which had shone in her eyes down in the car.

Olaf became afraid of them. At the same time he was angry at himself for having asked Gudrun that stupid question about going to bed. Go to bed just when Grete was struggling most! Of course no one wanted to. He was so busy thinking about that that he did not notice that the sounds from the bedroom had changed character. But then the midwife was in the doorway, hurrying to the kitchen.

'It's all over!' she called out.

Olaf glowed. Gudrun, too. Sissel came on the run and gave the midwife all the hot water she wanted.

The woman in the chair did not move.

'Did you hear that!' Sissel bubbled guilelessly at her.

The fluttery man cleared his throat and stepped forward.

'You see – ' he began, but Gudrun was over him, pulling at him, beside herself with joy and gratitude.

'Come outside, Dad! I've got something to tell you!' she shouted and simply pulled him out of the room, onto the porch, and was gone.

Sissel ran out to the kitchen again.

Olaf stood in the middle of the room, a bit confused. He had felt the rush of life from a new direction.

11

GUDRUN WAS GONE. No sooner was she out of sight than he began to doubt that she was really there, that she really had come and blessed his existence and looked deep into his eyes.

'Well, boy?' he heard beside him.

He straightened up. He had never heard anything like that voice, he thought as soon as he heard it, but then it belonged to the woman who sat imprisoned in the chair. She who had forced him to give his support to her.

Now she was alone in the room with him and was no longer dumb. She motioned to him.

'Come over here.'

He went over, but not willingly, there was nothing good awaiting him.

She glanced quickly at him and said in a hushed voice, so that it would not be heard in the bedroom:

'We've got to hurry now before the others come and make everything impossible.'

'With what?'

'Now I want you to promise again to be on my side. You've got to be on my side in everything that happens tonight.'

'What are we going to do, then?'

He was swept along by her mysterious tone of voice. He was a bit frightened, too, but did not want to miss the excitement she offered him.

'It's only now that I can talk,' she said without answering his question. 'I've told you what has happened. But he's hinted at much more and you've got to help me and save me from it.'

Now there gleamed and shone something in her eyes that he did not understand. He felt perplexed and helpless.

'But I can't,' he said desperately. 'Can't you talk with any of them? With Gudrun?'

She shook her head.

'I can't talk with any of them who were in the car and heard us. He'll get what he wants. I mean: he always gets what he wants. Once he wished that I would never be able to move off the spot again. And I haven't, either, ever since – except when he's carried me. I *have* to be that way! You don't understand that. You've only seen and heard him a little while.'

Olaf was not able to say a word. He sat still, horrified at her words. Timidly he waited for something: that she would also get up and walk.

He waited in vain. But she motioned with her finger for him to come closer.

'We can't let them hear us. He'll get just what he wants. Oh, I don't know, either,' she said suddenly. 'I feel so bad sometimes. I'm sorry for a lot of things, but – now and then I'm almost ready to call to him and tell him the truth. But as soon as I see him, I decide he can get just exactly what he wants. Then I think he can always get just what he wants. But now I'm safer, now that you're here if something happens.'

'I don't understand any of this,' Olaf said, still feeling just as helpless. 'I can't do anything.'

'We'll see,' she answered mysteriously. 'I'm not so sure of that. But if it becomes necessary tonight, you'll help me. Won't you?'

He could not answer. She held him fast with her eyes:

'No one's on my side, you see. Won't you?'

'I can't,' he stammered out and felt the invisible burden she was about to cast over him.

She just said:

'It's only some one like you who can. I can see well enough that you're just a kid, but just the same. From adults I've received so many disappointments. And you will come when I call for you, won't you?'

'Yes, I will,' he said firmly and glanced quickly at the door to the bedroom. But no one had heard.

Here was something new that had found its way to him. Not really so new, but something so different. Oh-ho, everything that happens to me! he thought. The same old thought. Actually he wanted to put his hands behind his back and make secret signs. Oh, don't be silly.

The woman's eyes were fastened on him unwaveringly. He thought she was beautiful. She had a fine strength in her eyes and in her voice and in the few movements she made with her arms.

She said:

'He's planned something for tonight. That's why you have to be ready to come when I call.'

Olaf jumped when he heard that. Maybe she was crazy after all. He shuddered, but was caught up by the words, by the stream of mystery flowing from her. She sat there beautiful and captive. He nodded stiffly that he was with her.

But he still made one exception:

'Not Gudrun.'

'What about her?'

'Gudrun's not a part of it.'

Gudrun must not become an enemy. The others were in a way enemies he had to be on guard against. But not Gudrun. No, not Grete or Karl, either, for that matter, not yet. But no matter what happened, not Gudrun.

'Oh, Gudrun – ' said the woman and smiled. 'Have you told me your name?'

'Yes. Olaf.'

'Yes, that's right. My name is Kristine. The rest of it is un-important, you're not going to get better acquainted with me – I almost hope. You're just going to help me in an emergency since we happened to stop right by your house. If you want to know the truth, I'm scared half stiff. No, you can't understand that before I've told you more about it, of course. And I guess I'll have to do that. It's getting closer – '

Olaf whispered quickly:

'Someone's coming.'

The handle on the bedroom had rattled. But then it stopped and was silent again.

The woman said softly:

'But they'll be coming soon now. So we'll have to talk later. When I'm in the room I've been promised and I call for you. I have to talk with someone, don't you see? I just have to!'

'Yes,' said Olaf, carried along. 'Shall I go now?'

'Wait a bit. I'm so lonely. I want – oh, no. It's my own fault. But wait just a bit.'

Olaf remained standing. Noises of joyful confusion came from the bedroom.

'Look here, Olaf,' she said and took a ring from her finger. 'This is what they used to do in the old days.'

'What?'

'You take this. It's just a token.'

He was entranced by her soft voice – and by her giving away something she owned like that.

He took it.

'Yes – ' he said breathlessly.

'But nobody is to know about it.'

'No.'

'There, now you've taken it from me.'

Everything that happens to me! he thought and slipped the ring into his pocket.

She said:

'Now it will be more difficult for you to forget when I call for you tonight.'

He heard it as a distant murmuring. He felt he had become more grown-up when he took the ring. Now he was really a part of it, he thought. Sissel could just go ahead and be big and have a sweet-heart she put her head together with – she wasn't part of anything like this.

The woman said:

'You see, I don't think there'll be any sleep for anyone in this house tonight.'

Did it sound threatening? Disturbing? No. Something else. Exciting and tempting. To be a part of it. He looked out into the dim, but still light, evening. It was late evening and the rain had stopped. The sky had risen now, but it was still clouded over. Everything beneath it lay in a paled light. The light of a June night. Men with pale cheeks are coming across the meadow and no one knows what has happened, ran through his mind. It was part of the strange mood he was in.

No, there aren't either, but look at that soft light now that the rain has stopped –

Then his thoughts made a sudden leap: If Tore's sitting in the bushes waiting for Sissel, he sure is wet! I just bet he is, he was so strange this evening. And no one is going to sleep around here tonight. Now it's going to begin. Oh-ho, he thought.

The woman asked wearily:

'See anybody out there?'

'No, nobody. Just that the rain has stopped. Nobody else is coming this evening. There's no one home but my sister and me.'

She shook herself sharply:

'Oh, I wish – ' she began. But it stopped and came to nothing.

'What?' he asked as calmly as he could. What what! he said impatiently inside himself.

'Don't be so impatient,' she answered. 'We'll talk later.'

The door handle rattled. She said quickly:

'And not a word now, Olaf.'

'No.'

She straightened up in the chair. Dumb once more.

12

WAS IT GOING to begin already? Olaf felt ready to help all he could. How, he did not know. That was to be seen. It was as if everything were possible this evening.

It was the fluttery man, Hjalmar, who came in. The enemy itself. But he was not aware of being an enemy at that moment. He was with Gudrun and was infected by the joy in the room with Grete. He came eagerly over to the chair.

'Soon we can go in and see!' he said. 'I'll get Karl and we'll carry you in.'

She made no sign of response. The man paid no attention to what she did.

'Grete's happy now!' he continued. 'And of course she wants to see you, too. And you've got to see the baby.'

He whirled around a couple of times as he said that. She sat in the chair unmoving and distant. Stiffened. It was creepy: Olaf had seen how she had stiffened when the man had appeared in the doorway. It sort of came by itself and took hold of her.

'Just this time?' he pleaded. But it was easy to hear that he was frightened. He did not dare wait for what she might reply, but called:

'Karl! Come in here.'

He called unnecessarily loudly and noisily. Karl came immediately. He was so happy that despite his strained face he showed it. Olaf stood in a way on guard against the enemy, but there appeared to be no danger now. The man said quickly to Karl:

'Shouldn't we carry her in so that she can see?'

'Yes, we can go in now,' replied Karl.

At last they were allowed to enter the room.

They got ready to take their usual hold on Kristine. The woman looked quickly at Olaf at the same instant and Olaf took it as a signal to him. He stepped in their way:

'No, don't touch her!' he said with failing courage, for he thought it was senseless to try to stop them from doing what they intended to do now. But he had promised blindly to stand by her, without question.

Karl's face tensed:

'What?'

'Go away!' said Olaf blindly.

But then all his backing was gone, for he saw the woman shaking her head at him. He had made a mistake. At the same time Karl said sharply:

'What business of yours is this, kid?'

The older man fluttered and blustered and buzzed in between Karl's words:

'He doesn't mean it. It's something else. He's not against us. Don't you see that Kristine – '

Karl shoved Olaf aside and the two men lifted the woman quickly. She just let them. Olaf felt cheated and stood waiting for a signal from her. No signal came. The door opened again and Gudrun steered in – straight at Olaf:

'Come on!'

The men had just disappeared inside with Kristine.

'You, too,' said Gudrun.

Then they were all collected in the parents' bedroom. The room was full – but still it was somehow as if only Grete's face filled it. A beaming from Grete. For the first time Olaf got a good look at her.

The newborn tiny creature snuffed untidily somewhere and caught its breath.

'Just like a little star,' someone in the room said suddenly.

They turned: it was the miserable, worn-out flutterer who had said that.

'For us,' he added when he noticed their eyes on him and then ducked in among the others.

Olaf was watching for signals, but was given nothing to do. Lights were burning in the room. Although it was light outside, it was still dim enough inside that the lamps cast a gleam around themselves. The dumb woman sat on a new chair and saw everything and nothing, her husband flitted around and chattered wearyingly and was forgiven immediately. Karl laughed proudly and wonderingly, and Gudrun laughed proudly at Olaf. The midwife stood there satisfied and factual.

Olaf somehow lost all backing for his defensiveness. The whole matter must have been postponed. The woman sat as if she rested. Olaf could now surrender himself to what he felt was the night's real magic.

13

OVER TO GUDRUN –

Frowsy-top up in the window – he did not know how many years he had talked with her there. She had been there and she had gradually changed her personality and ways of behaving with the passing years. As soon as he knocked on the wall she leaned out, bursting with pent-up laughter. When his mother and father had an argument and he went outside to avoid listening to it – then she and her lock of hair were a great consolation. Or when Sissel began acting too cocky. Or when no one had said anything and no one had done anything – and not least of all then.

But now a living and glistening Gudrun was standing down on earth. There in the corner. It was almost incomprehensible. But still, it was real. On that enchanted evening he could simply reach out with his hand and touch her, touch her thin, summer-bare arm.

She jumped when he did it.

'What do you want ?' she asked quickly.

'Nothing.'

'No.'

Their eyes rested in each other's a moment.

'Let's go outside!' he said, without knowing what they would do there.

'In the rain?'

'It stopped raining a long time ago. Haven't you even noticed that?'

She looked out of the window, where there was only the night's pale light.

'That's funny,' she said weakly.

He did not know what she thought was funny about it, he was trembling slightly and pulled at her arm. Gudrun followed him without resisting.

Out of the humming bedroom, out of the old house on quiet, hurrying feet. The air outside was fresh and there was a strange light that had lain in waiting in back of the rain. Now it spread itself out and would last the whole night.

The light-filled nights would soon be at their lightest and were full of warm, still cheeks.

Gudrun walked along beside him with still cheeks because it was night. Olaf saw it and knew that it was the same with him.

'What'll we do?' she asked when they reached the yard.

'Just walk. Shan't we?'

'Sure,' she said.

'Golly, it's strange,' she said again.

The night-long light.

'You've seen it before.'

'Not like this evening,' she said – or was it just something he thought she had said?

They walked down the road, came to an open grove that looked out over wide meadows. The mist lay like a thin veil over everything, and disappeared if one came closer.

'Shall we go out there?' he asked.

'No,' she said quickly.

But she stood bewitched by the sight.

Gudrun from up in the window down on earth. He mustn't say anything about that. Just hold her arm. He also had a burning desire to find out how her lock of hair smelled. A tiny hint of it swept past him.

'Let me,' he said and bent forward.

'What ?'

'See if your hair smells good.'

She smiled at his demand. Was quiet and serious.

'Sure, go ahead.'

'Don't you expect it to smell like other hair ?' she continued, but without grinning, as he could have expected.

She bent forward. Her hair fell down around her face.

He smelled it. Could not discover anything special about its odor. For him it was a great experience. The fragrance of her hair came toward him like the meadow mist up from the earth, swept past as if it were nothing, and was gone.

'Finished ?' she asked and stood bent over with her head toward him.

'Yes.'

He took a deep breath.

'Are you fourteen ?' he asked.

'No, I'm thirteen.'

'Oh – '

He became happy in a new way. Felt wonderful inside in a new way. But he really ought not to stand there too long, he had promised to stay close to the woman in the chair. But he should be allowed to stand there a little while.

Gudrun tossed her hair back again, and was silent. Looked at him with her dark eyes. Those dark eyes made her unfamiliar and somehow did not agree with the invisible image he had known. Maybe she would soon say something – something unfamiliar, too – something that would turn many things upside down when it came out.

He asked tensely:

'Well, what are you waiting for?'

She was puzzled.

'Waiting for?'

'Yes, to say sort of – '

'Nothing at all,' she said and grinned.

'No – ' he said, but saw very clearly that it was not entirely true. Now Gudrun took the initiative:

'But you, then? What is it you want?'

'We've got to go back in now,' he said shyly, since this was so much different from being near Sissel, sensing a fragrance from Sissel, seeing Sissel.

She said in an unsteady voice:

'It's not raining any longer, so as far as that's concerned – '

That set him back a bit. What should he answer to that? And on the spur of the moment! But she was the quicker:

'But now we have to go back in,' she said loudly.

'Yes, so that we can find out what they're doing,' answered Olaf in the same tone of voice. A firm, saving tone.

They went across the yard side by side. And chanced to hold each other's hand. Firm, lonely hands that suddenly had something strange to hold. The meadow still lay there playing with its veil of mist and the pale light was on the road and the trees and on every cheek. Thus it was, amid a fragrance from Gudrun.

14

THE LIVING ROOM WAS far from empty now. All who did not absolutely have to be in the bedroom, had once again been chased out. The silent woman, Kristine, had once more been placed in the armchair by the radio. Hjalmar stood and twiddled the knobs on the radio and tapped small squirts and gushes of music or words. Karl was leaning against the wall doing nothing. But his expression was still not completely free and happy. From the kitchen, on the other hand, came glad sounds: the door was open and Sissel could be seen bustling around preparing food while she hummed gaily.

Olaf took measure of the people. The enemy. He received no signal from Kristine in the chair.

'Stay here,' he said to Gudrun and deposited her, so to speak, as far as possible from Kristine. He himself went over to the chair and casually took his position at the woman's right hand.

She gave him a rapid glance. So the connection was in order.

What now?

The fluttering father immediately descended upon Gudrun in his restless journey around the floor.

'What became of you, anyway, Gudrun? You just went right out and left it all. Aren't you interested in it? Don't you think it's something special? Isn't it raining anymore? Why don't you answer?'

Gudrun nodded to him.

She certainly knew from many times before how much use it was answering into that confused flow. The man stopped chattering and smiled at her instead.

'We were really afraid for Grete a while back in the car, weren't we?'

Gudrun nodded.

'But now everything's fine,' he said. Then he began stammering: 'Yes, that is – you see, that is – oh, nothing.'

His eyes were constantly flitting around the room and his hands were never still.

It was difficult for Olaf to imagine that he was a protector against this helpless and wearying man, but he had to keep his promise in mind. It would soon be night – when the woman expected almost anything.

The man stopped right in front of her.

'Kristine,' he said, 'you're right in this with us, too. I can see that.'

His nervous fingers played with the knee of his trousers as he talked. All eyes in the room were turned on Kristine. As soon as she noticed it her face became tenser. She made no more of it than that. The man stood in front of her and was obviously screwing up his courage.

'And you're glad to be here, too, Kristine. To see it all, right in the middle of everything we're struggling with. I guess you've looked forward to it most of all!'

He certainly meant it as some kind of concession to her – that could be heard in his tone of voice – but he did not succeed in breaking through with it, it fell to earth.

He then lost control and became frightened.

'You could at least admit it!' he shouted, he who so recently had wished that she were dumb and as punishment had had his wish fulfilled.

Now it must be beginning. Olaf stood ready, turned toward the unknown. He looked at Kristine, who had asked for help, screwed up his courage, stepped forward and with half-paralyzed tongue shot out:

'She can't answer.'

The man took a couple of steps backwards and his face flushed. He looked quickly at the woman, then turned toward Olaf. Olaf stood as straight as he could.

Karl had also heard and came over. He was not afraid of Olaf, took a firm hold on his shoulder and said angrily:

'Just who do you think you are, anyway? Get away from here!'

Olaf shook with fear – for something wild and hard had come into Karl's face and a thought shot through him: the war – . But he still managed to stammer:

'This is my house – '

It was as if Karl had received a blow across the nose. He stopped short and mumbled something.

Gudrun called from the background:

'Olaf, don't butt in!'

With that she began to cry. The lock of her hair fell forward. So overwrought and under strain as she was. Olaf did not have the slightest idea of what he should do. Karl stood in front of him with an unpleasant hardness over him. Kristine sat there in the chair as if she heard nothing. The fluttery man writhed and complained:

'Oh, what a mess!'

It occurred to Olaf that this man had wished misfortune upon another human being. He felt sorry for him, but could do nothing. Punishment is not sweet.

Karl said, annoyed:

'What's a mess? That Grete and I have gotten a son? And that everything has turned out unbelievably well compared to how it looked just a little while ago? It doesn't seem to me that there's any mess here right now.'

Olaf moved so that he touched the arm of the woman he was guarding.

The man in the middle of the room just whined on:

'A mess, a mess – '

Olaf felt uncomfortable. Of Gudrun he saw only the forward fallen lock of hair. Just a short while before he had buried his face in it and felt it around him. Now he stood there bewildered.

The woman beside him began to move: she grasped the arms of the chair and pulled herself up. She stood there, rigidly supporting herself with her arms, and looked searchingly at those around her.

What did she mean by it? The others stood as if they were thinking: Watch out now! What are you going to do? Don't! The two men were ready to jump forward. Olaf flamed up: now he saw his enemies, he saw red and screamed viciously at them:

'Leave her alone! It's you who've made her dumb!'

'She isn't,' said Karl calmly.

The older man flapped and whined:

'A mess – oh – '

Olaf's shout had brought Sissel to the kitchen door. The door had been closed a while now, but Sissel had still heard. She came running in and grabbed Olaf so that it shook him from head to toe:

'Have you gone crazy? What are you doing, anyway? Are you going to start fighting with these people?'

Then he realized that he was standing holding a footstool over his head, aimed at Karl.

'Get away, you don't know anything about this!' he hissed, but let the stool sink peacefully down.

Sissel was no weakling, and she dragged Olaf out of the room. He managed to catch a glimpse of Kristine sinking down into the chair again, saw her husband buzzing around, saw the lovely lock of hair lying as before, hiding shame and sorrow – then he was pushed into the kitchen. Sissel closed the door firmly.

'What's gotten into you?' she asked.

He shook his head.

'Maybe you don't want to tell me?' she asked again, and it was no gentle question.

Olaf squirmed a bit.

'It's nothing for you to get worried about. I've just promised to help out with something.'

'Help out by hitting people?'

'By doing just anything that's necessary,' he answered excitedly. 'That's just what I've promised.'

'Her in the chair?'

'Yes.'

'You've promised – ' she began, but he took it away from her, nodded to her as to a child:

'I know quite a bit more than you do now, Sissel. So you can just lay off me.'

Sissel laughed.

'Well, you'll have to tell me more if I'm going to understand any of it. But you just can't stand like that waving footstools at people.'

'You wouldn't laugh if you knew what I know.'

'Pooh.'

Then it occurred to him that this was the first time they had been alone together since it all had come tumbling down on them.

'It turned out a bit different than we thought it would this evening!'

65

'Yes, it sure did,' answered Sissel happily.

'What are you so happy about?'

Sissel gave no answer.

He understood well enough that it was because of Grete and her baby; he had caught a glimpse of Sissel's shining face in there before.

There it came:

'It's nothing that boys can understand. So it doesn't mean anything to you,' she said. 'But now tell me what you've gotten yourself mixed up in.'

Should he keep it to himself? He was no longer frightened by it. Now that he was with Sissel he felt how the excitement rippled through him. He felt as if he were on top of rolling events and at the same time felt his own strength growing.

'I don't really know very much about it,' he had to admit. 'The woman sitting in the chair is dumb – but she can talk to me. And I'm to stand by her if necessary tonight.'

Sissel stared at him.

'If necessary tonight? What sort of nonsense is that? It's all over now. But that's just like you, Olaf; you go making things up until you believe them yourself and then go charging off like a bull in a china shop.'

'I'll help you, too, if it's necessary,' he said in playful arrogance and cut her off.

Sissel jumped as if she had been stuck. Then she laughed.

'Thanks. I'll let you know. But now look here,' she said in a different tone of voice, 'no more talking nonsense. Where are all these people going to sleep tonight. They'll have to stay here.'

'They're not going to sleep,' Olaf could inform her.

'Of course they're going to sleep. But we don't have enough beds for them all. Don't know if there's enough food, either.'

Nothing is needed tonight, he thought, full of the coming hours. Food? Beds? What difference did that make?

'They'll have to use our beds, Olaf. And then we'll see. But now they've got to eat,' she said with her nose in cupboards and drawers, and there was happiness in her voice.

'Do you know what her husband said to her,' she continued.

'Karl?'

'Yes – If you had only heard what he said to Grete in the bed-room – '

'Shhh!'

A crash from something striking the floor sounded from the living room. They jumped. Olaf said immediately, frightened:

'It's Karl. He was in the war and was – '

'The war?' repeated Sissel. Fear flamed through the room. Olaf was already on the way in, with his heart in his throat.

'What are you going to do?'

'I've promised to stand by if – you come, too!'

It all happened quickly. Olaf tore open the door and charged in. Sissel followed close on his heels.

The footstool lay right in front of their feet, buckled in two and with one leg broken off. But no one was hurt or injured. Karl stood in the middle of the room and it was clearly he who had thrown the stool so hard. Karl looked stern and dark. Perhaps even darker than he really was – when you knew that he had been injured in the war. His bewildered father had squeezed himself into a corner.

Gudrun pulled at her brother:

'Karl! Stop it now!'

The midwife opened the bedroom door and peeked out.

Olaf glanced quickly at Kristine to see if she would signal to him. No, nothing now, either. He told himself that she was pleased that he had come, anyway. He stopped near her.

Karl picked up the footstool and the broken leg. Stood turning it over in his hands.

'You'll have to excuse me, Dad,' he said and tried to get control over his voice, 'but now and then it's just too much for a mere human being to have to see and hear you. For me it is, anyway. All I ask is that you stop chattering unendingly and fluttering around un-endingly.'

He stopped. Turned the stool over and over in his hands. Olaf saw that it had nothing to do with the woman in the chair. The older man in the corner supported himself against the wall and wiped his face.

'I know it, I know it,' he mumbled.

Gudrun's voice rose up through it:

'But he really is nice!'

Then she noticed that Olaf had come in. She went over to him and took his arm.

'He really is nice,' she said stubbornly.

Olaf became soft and kind inside.

'Yes,' he said.

Kristine looked sharply at him and he became embarrassed over what he had said.

Sissel stepped right into it all and said as if nothing had happened:

'Everyone come into the kitchen now and get something to eat.'

What?

They all stopped short. Food? Then they eagerly grasped at it. Karl looked at Sissel so that she blushed and became nervous.

'Thank you,' he said and looked at her as if he had not noticed her before.

Gudrun said clearly and proudly on behalf of Olaf, so that all should be sure of it:

'Is that your sister?'

It was easy for Olaf to say 'yes' to that at the moment – Sissel had made out well when she stepped into the middle of all the conflict.

Sissel turned her back to Karl and said to Kristine:

'There's food for all. I'll bring you a tray. All you others come along now. How about in there?' she asked the midwife, who was still standing in the half-open doorway to the bedroom. 'Are they sleeping? I'll bring something in later.'

Sissel hurried around and arranged everything. The midwife just nodded and closed the door. Sissel opened the kitchen door wide and quickly hurried them in, as if she were afraid something new would break loose.

'Well, that's sure nice of you, but – . We're really not hungry, but – . Who can eat now ?' fluttered Hjalmar and followed the others in.

Olaf was left alone with Kristine. He looked after Sissel in amazement.

15

As SOON AS THE KITCHEN DOOR was closed, Kristine made a dissatisfied movement. Olaf expected it. He knew that he had not behaved as she had wanted him to.

'Well ?' she said skeptically, in that half-whispering tone of voice they always had to use.

Yes, he expected a scolding.

'I just don't know how much you're to be depended on for help, Olaf. What will you do in a real crisis ?'

It hurt him to hear that. Had he already broken his promise ? He really did not think so, but perhaps he could have been a bit harsher toward the nervous man – but he just couldn't be.

'Gudrun is not included,' he said firmly. 'We agreed on that. Nobody has to be scared of her.'

She stamped a little on the floor.

'Scared ? Who's talking about being scared ? I'm not.'

It occurred to him that she looked very scared. But it was not long before she twisted it around:

'It's he who's scared to death. You've certainly seen that this evening.'

'Yes,' answered Olaf and felt fear creeping up and down his own spine.

She shook her head.

'You just agree with everything I say.'

A discarded habit crept forth: he hid his hands behind his back to make magic signs.

'What are you doing now?'

He stretched his empty hands out in front of him.

They whispered. Not a sound must reach the kitchen. Through the kitchen door they could clearly hear the voices of Sissel and Gudrun.

'Shall I go?' he asked, with a feeling of being rejected.

'Don't you have my ring in your pocket? Why did I give it to you? You're not getting off that easy.'

'But I don't know what I'm supposed to do! And I'm sure I couldn't do it anyway.'

'You can do more than you realize. Everybody can.'

He was silent, felt a warmness from her words and believed in them. She said:

'There's a lot I have to tell you. I have to have someone to talk to. Someone who's not involved. I just can't stand listening to him!' she began without any introduction. 'Maybe I'm not like other people – at any rate, I can become so sick of him that I can say terrible things, and do terrible things. In the car today I was nasty and he got mad and said that he wished that I would never be able to say another word. Yes, I'm sure I've told you that before, but you can listen to it again. As soon as he said that I just had to let him get what he wished for.'

'No!' whispered Olaf, frightened.

'And now he's scared to death that it's for good. You see for yourself how he is. But I can't take it back! Can't take anything back!'

A question was implied in this, for Olaf: had she made herself lame, too? But he dared not ask it. It was something dark not to be touched.

Suddenly she said:

'I'm so sorry I don't know what to – '

Olaf started, it came so unexpectedly. Should he answer that? Was it said to him? He had to turn away – it was embarrassing to be a witness to such a confession.

She continued:

'But I just can't say that to him. He makes it impossible.'

Olaf remained silent. She had to call to him:

'Did you hear what I said?'

'Yes.'

'I need to tell you many things. You'll just have to be so kind as to listen.'

'When?' he asked and wished that he were far away from her.

'I don't know. Could be right now, for that matter. No, come to me later.'

'Yes,' he promised. She said:

'I'm tired, too, Olaf.'

'But is it that way with all of them?' he asked on Gudrun's behalf. 'That you can't talk with them?'

She nodded.

'I see that you're also tired, Olaf.'

Yes, he felt that he was dead tired. It was late evening now, he was used to being asleep by this time.

Sissel came out of the kitchen with a tray, pushed a small table over beside Kristine's chair and said:

'Here's something for you to eat.'

Kristine nodded in thanks and began picking at the food. Sissel turned to Olaf:

'Come out to the kitchen now and get something to eat, you too. The others are almost finished.'

'Don't want any.'

'Why not?'

'I'm not hungry.'

Sissel shrugged her shoulders, a bit irritated, but then she saw how tired he was and became friendlier toward him.

'You look like you need some sleep. But it – ' she stopped. 'Lie down on the sofa here, Olaf,' she continued, and was only gentle with him now. Then she returned quickly to the kitchen.

From the kitchen could be heard a steady flow of talking, or rather, a buzzing. It was easy to know who was making it.

Dead tired. Because it was so long past his usual bedtime, but also because of the tension that now temporarily had slackened. He knew that there was no danger now. No one would be hurt tonight. Relaxation hit him with double force. He lay down on the roomy, worn sofa and stretched out.

The woman watched him as she ate and asked softly:

'Is it my fault that you can't eat anything?'

'Leave me alone,' he pleaded, a little dazed. He felt sleep creeping heavily through him and could offer no resistance – for it had been a hard evening.

'Just go to sleep,' she said. 'I'll be able to wake you when I need you.'

He settled himself comfortably, blinked several times. Then he knew no more.

16

OLAF WAS WAKENED by something sweet and fragrant falling over him. He realized while still half asleep that it was Gudrun bending over him. He had never wakened like that before.

'Goodnight, Olaf,' she said. 'It's Gudrun.'

Goodnight? Oh, yes, of course, it wasn't morning, it was just later in the evening.

'Goodnight, Gudrun,' he answered with a slow yawn. It just came out; he really was not sure if Gudrun had said goodnight to him at all. Sissel must have gotten things arranged. Oh, sure, she was to sleep in his room –

'Has Sissel fixed you up?'

'Yes, and you know what? I'm going to sleep in your bed! I didn't want to chase you out, but she said I should sleep there. Goodnight now, Olaf.'

'Mmmm – wait a minute,' he said and he was not yet awake enough to answer properly. He looked up into her face, sighed in satisfaction and was on the point of dropping off again. The lamp was on in the room, but it looked as if it were lighter outside. Then that was all. Gudrun crept away.

But there were other people in the room, he was not given a chance to fall asleep again so quickly. Sissel came over to him. She was wide awake and pleased with herself, shoved at him a bit in order to make room for herself beside him and crept onto the sofa.

'Well, now they're all tucked away,' she sighed lightly after a job well done. 'Raise up a bit, so that I can get the blanket out from under you. We can put it over us. We'll sleep here– if we can get any sleep. The midwife is sleeping in with Grete, in Dad's bed. We carried that creepy one in the chair into my room and your little sweetheart has to sleep in your room – see ?'

'But Karl and – '

'I put them up in the attic, on the old divan up there,' Sissel said, and Olaf could hear that she liked mentioning them. 'Anyone who goes around throwing footstools has to sleep up there.'

'Who did the carrying ?'

'The two men, of course. They looked like they'd had plenty of practice at it.'

'What did she say ?'

'Say ? She didn't say anything, of course.'

'No, of course not. Golly! Our folks sure ought to see their house now!' he added quickly.

'It's good they can't. And good they weren't home when this happened. But now it's fun! Since it turned out so well for Grete,' she said.

'Boy, you sure stared at Karl!'

'I did not!' Sissel replied angrily.

He lay on the sofa beside Sissel. He pinched her lightly and liked her. The blanket was too warm for that weather and slipped to the floor. Somehow it was not the same Sissel as earlier in the evening, when they were down in the field with the snails. Something was different.

'You sure perked up when you were wished goodnight just now, Olaf. You were sleeping like a rock while we were clattering around here getting things arranged. Now you'd better go to sleep again.'

'No, I'm not going to sleep any more tonight,' he said. 'I'm wide awake now. Do you think you're going to get any sleep?'

'Not as long as I lie here, I won't.'

'No, on account of something else.'

'Oh?'

'I don't think anybody's going to get any sleep tonight,' he said and gradually became as awake as in the middle of the day. 'I'm pretty sure a lot's going to happen.'

'That sounded somber,' said Sissel and sighed sorrowlessly, threw her arm over him and lay her head against him to go to sleep. She said drowsily:

'We're too tired to play all your games now, Olaf. Now we're going to sleep. Goodnight.'

She cuddled down.

He was glad that Sissel had come and wanted to sleep beside him like that. She felt heavy and lifeless now. Sissel who was so full of life. Then his thoughts fell on Gudrun. *She* surely wasn't asleep. He could have gone in and held her hand. And he could have sat like that until morning, he thought.

He lay awake, on watch for a thumping to sound through the house. That would be a signal from the woman in Sissel's room. The door to both that room and his own room opened onto the hall – so he would first have to go out into the hall to reach her. But he would be able to hear her signal through the walls. Soon she would knock on the floor. It was certain that she was not asleep. It was too bad that he had been asleep when they had carried her out – that hadn't looked too good, he was her guard. Now he would just have to wait for the thumping –

'Look, Sissel,' he whispered, right in the middle of a stream of thought.

Sissel was not asleep – she immediately lifted her head. Olaf pointed out the window, out into the still, warm night.

'What do you see?'

'I don't see anything. It's just so strange out there.'

He wanted to look some more, but she pulled him down.

'It's not very nice of you to make such a racket when somebody's trying to sleep,' she said in the same satisfied tone of voice as before. 'There. Like that. Now go to sleep, Olaf.'

It was light outside. A faint, peaceful night light lay over the countryside, over the meadow full of mist, over the angelica with their bristling shades of blossoms, over the tufts of grass with their mysteries. Can't you see it all, Sissel? he thought. I wonder if Tore's still wandering around out there? ran through his mind – as he felt Sissel's body beside him, heavy and full of sleep.

17

THEY BOTH SAT UP:

A door had opened somewhere in the house.

'Didn't I say so?' whispered Olaf. 'No one's sleeping tonight.'

'Shhh. That's probably just the man who can never keep still. Up in the attic. That must be him wandering around.'

'Or it could be the one who was in the war, too,' whispered Olaf. 'Have you taken a good look at him, Olaf?'

'What do you mean?'

'No, nothing.'

They sat listening to the wandering in the attic. It was unpleasant to listen to. Otherwise there was not a sound in the house. Outside it was light. The air in the living room felt heavy and warm.

'Now he's coming down.'

The footsteps came stealthily down the stairs. But they were old stairs and in the stillness of the night each step creaked. Now the man was down in the hall. The door handle began turning slowly. The slower it was turned, the more it squeaked. Soon the man would be there.

Sissel jumped up.

'I'm going out!' she whispered. 'I don't want to stay here.'

'Why not?'

'It must be him – the one who was in the war. I don't want to meet him – '

She had kicked off her shoes when she had crept onto the sofa, now she picked them up and ran out into the kitchen – and made it in time. Whoever it was turning the door handle was slowed down by the screeching of the unoiled catch.

Olaf lay on the sofa in the same position as before. But his heart beat unsteadily.

It was not Karl after all who came in, but his restless father.

He stood just inside the door and looked around quickly. He was fully dressed, had undoubtedly not had a single stitch of clothing off. He started when he saw Olaf.

'Oh!' he said, confused. 'Pardon me.'

Olaf got to his feet.

'Is there anything wrong?' he asked quickly.

'Are you in here?' said the man surprised. 'Oh, sure, that's right. But how was I to know? I didn't recognize the door. I thought it was – no, I don't know, I happened to – no, that's all, I'll leave.'

'Who did – ' began Olaf.

'No one!' the man cut in. 'I see that now that I'm here. It wasn't really a mistake. Oh, my God, if only someone could tell me – let me by, I've got to get out!'

'Are you going to hurt her some more?' asked Olaf numbly.

The man jumped:

'What are you talking about?'

Olaf regretted his words and wanted to try to cover up somehow, but he was not quite sure how he could twist them around, nor was he even given a chance to get started – for the man sent a stream of words at him:

'Just what's going on in your mind, anyway? That's not why I'm here. On the contrary, if you want to know. And now that I think of it, you're just the person I've got to get hold of first of all. I feel like I'm walking in my sleep – I've got to get some information from you, as turned around as that may sound, from you who really don't have the slightest idea what we're struggling with. And then you go and think – just who do you think has it worst!' he concluded.

Olaf felt like saying: Well, go in there, then. It was easy to hear how the man wove himself into a net of self-contradictions and excuses – but it was clear that he had not come to hurt anyone. The man began again:

'You know very well why I have to talk to you. You've got to explain why you behaved like you did. The way you stood beside Kristine, what was the reason for that?'

Olaf was in trouble now. He wanted most of all to go into the kitchen with Sissel.

'You were even ready to fight,' said the man. 'Why?'

Olaf squirmed. How could he get out of this? The man kept pressing him now that he had first gotten hold:

'You stood there just as if you were defending Kristine against someone. Yes, against us others, of course.'

Olaf was silent.

'Have we done anything to you?'

'No.'

'But I've got to find out what you were defending Kristine against here in this house.'

'I don't know. Against everything!' said Olaf loudly and angrily, because he was at a loss for an answer.

'Shhh,' said the man, 'not so loud, it's the middle of the night. Don't shout. When did you two get to know each other, anyway?'

'When she was down in the car.'

The man said quickly:

'What did she do when you were down there alone with her?'

Olaf did not answer. What was this man after? He was dangerous, no matter how fluttery and wearying he was otherwise.

'Well?'

'I've heard that she was made dumb in the car,' said Olaf stiffly. Screwed up his courage all he could.

The man reacted as if he had been struck across the face.

'That's none of your business,' he said. 'You're just a kid – and a stranger as well.'

'I've been asked to help her and I've promised to,' answered Olaf and grew warm; he felt miserable, he felt only too well that he was just a kid. He pulled himself together.

'Who asked you to?'

Olaf did not want to admit that he had talked with her; he did not answer. And Gudrun wasn't going to be dragged into it. But as it turned out, he did not have to ponder over it very long, the man suddenly became frightened and did not wish to pursue the matter farther.

'Do you think this is a cross-examination?' he asked and flitted around. 'Oh, no, no, not at all. Am I bothering you? Everything I do just gets all turned around and upside down.'

When Olaf looked closely, he thought that the man was quite handsome, but pale and bewildered, and constantly plagued by fluttering and chattering.

'Everything I do,' he buzzed. 'You saw how Karl broke that footstool, just because he was sick and tired of me. Everybody gets that way. What can I do about it?'

Olaf shook his head. The man just kept talking:

'You're too young to answer me, I realize that. But can you just imagine how it must be to be me? Everything I want to do, I can't. I can't, I can't!'

He buzzed around, and then it came:

'Once I wished that she would never be able to use her feet again – '

'Oh ?' said Olaf and had to wet his lips.

'Everything I do goes wrong!' said the man. 'Nothing turns out right. But just exactly how did you get on her side ? I want to know! No, you're really not, you're just scared.'

Olaf was silent.

'If you're not scared, just say so!'

Olaf nodded.

Sure he was scared.

The house around them had the stillness of night over it. There was no way of knowing how many were asleep – but they were quiet, anyway. A short while before a faint cry had come from the new-born baby in the next room, but it had quickly died away.

The man wrung his hands and said:

'Just don't you go thinking that you understand Kristine. I saw how you stood there beside her, but you don't understand any of this.'

'No,' said Olaf.

'None of us has done you any harm.'

Olaf felt as if he had been put in his place, but the man ground on, so that he had no chance to think it over.

'You stood there waving the footstool, and just afterwards Karl stood there waving it. Against me alone. Everyone turns against me and nobody can stand me – '

He twisted and fluttered like a lost bird. Looked at Olaf to see if his words had had an effect. Looked out into the peaceful night on the other side of the window.

Olaf said:

'Gudrun can stand you.'

The man lit up in the middle of his misery and sat down.

'Did she tell you that ?'

'Yes.'

It was as if Gudrun had gotten out of bed and stood between them.

'Ah, yes, – without Gudrun – '

It did not last long.

A thumping sounded through the house.

A series of thumps on the floor somewhere in the house. They were abruptly called away from the vision of Gudrun's friendliness and strangeness. They both jumped.

'That's Kristine,' whispered the man and looked desperately at Olaf.

Olaf whispered:

'Yes, I know it.'

He fumbled to get his shoes on and tried to get his thoughts collected around what she could want.

'What does she want now?' whispered the man. 'That's a signal to me.'

But he did not go. Then he noticed what Olaf was doing.

'What are you going to do?' he asked sharply.

'That's a signal to me,' answered Olaf uneasily. 'I promised to come.'

'You? That's my wife who's knocking out the same signal she's used thousands of times this past year. Oh, thousands and thousands of times – '

'Well, that's still a signal to me,' Olaf stammered out. He was excited and raised his voice, was filled with apprehension, but started to go.

The man grabbed his arm with an unbelievably strong hand and held on.

'Just you stop now! That's for me. That thumping we just heard was for me, you can just be sure of that. You don't know her different signals.'

'No,' Olaf had to admit, 'I guess not.'

'Let's listen now, there'll be more.'

The thumping sounded again, the same number of thumps as the first time. Olaf had nothing against that. He could turn it over to the man.

Hjalmar stood there as if deserted and lonesome. He had been summoned. He began to shake.

'I've got to go in, but I don't dare,' he whispered. 'Not just now.

I'll do it tomorrow! My God! she'll just have to wait until tomorrow. Everything's so different at night, and so much worse.'

Olaf thought to himself: that's how it is to have made a person dumb. He wanted to go out to the kitchen and find Sissel. The man pleaded:

'Wait.'

'Why?'

'Oh, I don't know. Just to stall a bit – can't you help me find a way to stall a while?' he asked weakly.

The thumping sounded again. At the same instant the kitchen door was opened and Sissel stood there. She must have heard the thumping and could not stand it any longer.

'Don't you hear it?' she asked.

Olaf waved her away. She closed the door again.

'I'm going out a while,' the man said.

'What? When she's calling?'

The man's face reflected a great need.

'I really did intend to go in,' he confessed, 'but now that she's calling, I don't dare. Don't dare!' he buzzed. 'But tomorrow I will. I'm going out a while – '

Olaf could see how ashamed he was.

'Well, then, don't go far,' he said reluctantly.

'Will you help me?' asked the man.

'Help you?'

'Yes, I'm the one who needs help.'

Help him, too. Olaf did not know what to do or answer.

'Wh-what with?'

'What with?' the man said almost angrily. 'Just help me, of course. If I need it. It could be in many ways, just be ready for anything. I need your help! Will you?'

He flapped and it was unbearable to watch.

'Yes,' said Olaf in resignation. What am I doing? he thought. You promised her first.

'Well, I'm going,' said the man. 'Just going. But tomorrow – . Can't you see something's got to be done about this?'

He tumbled out of the door. Olaf watched him go through the yard, down the driveway toward the deserted car. He himself looked pathetically deserted.

Olaf jumped: the thumping again. But this time not the same as before.

Now it's for me –

Well, I've done her no harm, he encouraged himself with, and started to go.

Sissel came out again.

'What's that?'

'It's for me, not you.'

He gave no further explanation, summoned all his courage, went out into the hall and into Sissel's room.

18

SISSEL'S WELL-KNOWN ROOM. With the lamp burning on the small night table beside her pillow. How many times hadn't he come into this room on errands to Sissel?

Now the older and unknown woman Kristine lay there. Beside her stood her cane. She was alone, there was no one trying to hurt her, but her eyes shone from something impossible deep inside.

She waved to him.

He went to her immediately. He had shut the door.

'Why didn't Hjalmar come when I called for him?' she asked without any introduction.

'Don't know.'

'He heard it, that's for sure. He usually hears it no matter where he is. I want Hjalmar now, this is no good – '

Olaf did not dare ask what was no good. Her eyes glowed too much.

'Where is Hjalmar?'

'He left,' said Olaf. He said it like that in fear, and heard that it sounded hard.

'Left? He can't have!'

'He'll come back tomorrow,' Olaf hurried to add.

'Did he say that?'

'Yes.'

'Tomorrow. What do you know about tomorrow?'

'Nothing.'

'Well, then be still. Tomorrow? Leave me alone!' she said irritably. 'I'm so sorry that I don't know what – I've already told you that. Go away!'

He went toward the door. She raised her hand:

'But if I knock, then you've got to come. I can't know anything about – '

'Yes, yes,' he said and slipped out into the hall. Who should he listen to?

No one was in the living room. Sissel must still be in the kitchen. He opened the door. Yes, Sissel was sitting there, leaning against the wall sleeping. He banged around a bit, but she slept soundly. He himself was wide awake and excited. He thought of shaking her and telling her, but no, he let her be. She was sleeping with her mouth wide open like a child. He crept silently back into the living room.

He went past the bedroom door and heard a sound inside. A strange sound, it seemed to him, in his confused state of mind. He could not resist, he had to peek in.

19

ANOTHER WELL-KNOWN ROOM transformed in the magic night. Also here a lamp was burning in the gentle half-light.

The midwife was still on duty and had lain down fully dressed on one of the beds, ready to be called. Now she was sleeping, to all appearances soundly and peacefully. Golly, the way people sleep around here, he thought.

The baby lay there, asleep. It was impossible to know what had caused the sound.

But now only Grete mattered – the young woman who had given birth to a child in the middle of a journey and had landed in this strange and unfamiliar house. She must have gone to sleep after it all and just awakened now. At any rate, she was not sleeping and Olaf received a welcome he felt from head to toe.

She raised her arms as soon as he was inside the door. The light in the room made her arm still softer than it would have appeared in daylight – and the arm gently motioned to Olaf: in! come on in –

He did not need a second invitation, he closed the door and went toward the bed.

He looked over at the midwife, but she appeared to be sleeping deeply. He could concentrate on Grete.

When she had arrived earlier in the evening her face had been distorted by pain and fear. Now Olaf saw her face as it was when it was in a woman's heaven – and it had a powerful effect on him. He stopped short.

She made a motion for him to come closer. He went right up to her and looked deep into her eyes.

He had not made a sound yet, now Grete spoke and greeted him:

'It's fine that you finally came, too. Everyone else has been in to see me – I was anxious to find out what you would do, Olaf, for I know that's your name.'

She spoke very softly so that she would not wake the reassuring, solid woman in the other bed.

Her words did him good. Then she pointed at the baby:

'You're to look at it.'

Olaf nodded. Something small and dark lay on the pillow. He did not look very closely at it.

'You've got to take a better look than that, Olaf. You don't get off so easy. It's a wonderful thing, this here.'

He took another look, at the same time wondering about the sound he had heard. Had he been half asleep, after all? Grete said:

'Your sister doesn't think this is such an unimportant thing, either. Has she finally gotten a chance to rest a bit now? I guess we turned this house upside down tonight.'

'Ahh, that's all right,' he said.

She looked at him quickly, because of his tone of voice.

'It's just fine,' he added.

'You're a funny one,' she said, even more softly. 'Sit down.'

He sat down on the chair close to the pillow, so that he could clearly see that happy face. The child lying there had no effect on him, but she herself did.

'And you're a night owl, I see,' she said happily. As if that gave her pleasure, too.

'Oh, there's really no place to sleep.'

He shouldn't have said that. Grete answered quickly:

'Yes, there were so many of us who descended upon you. I'm awfully sorry. And that we've chased you out of your beds,' she finished, 'that's the worst of it.'

'No, that's all right.'

'And your sister has been so nice, too. I've only caught a glimpse or two of you through the door. Because when I arrived I didn't see too much. But Gudrun has told me a little about you – that your name is Olaf and all such. And this is Grete who has had a little boy.'

'Is that why you can't sleep?'

'Yes. It's really too bad that you'll never be able to try this.'

'It didn't sound like it was so terribly much fun – '

'I've forgotten all that now, Olaf. Do you know where Sissel is?' she asked suddenly.

'She was sitting in the kitchen sleeping just before I came in here.'

'Poor kid.'

'But that Butterfly has gone out.'

'Oh, what's the matter now ? Did you notice anything about him ?'

'He left when she knocked on the floor. He'll see her in the morning.'

Grete took his arm.

'Yes, Gudrun has told me that you've been dragged into that miserable business between them. I guess it was pretty bad when we were on the road this afternoon – I had enough to think about with myself so that I don't remember it very well, but – . Gudrun has told me a little bit about it now, so I know how serious it was.'

'When she was alone in the car – ' Olaf began, but she stopped him:

'Olaf. Stop right there. Gudrun has told you a few things – but now we can just let all that be and see if it doesn't pass over. As I lie here, I have the feeling somewhere inside me that a lot of things are going to be different now. Karl will be different and that will have its effect on the others. I don't think what happened in the car will make any difference now.'

Olaf suspected that it was her state of elation over the new-born child that formed her words. He felt it was good to surrender himself to them, and did so gladly. Her hand still rested on his arm.

Many kinds of loose thoughts raced through his mind. Stay, strange light. Stay, soft hand. Stay, lovely eyes. Women.

What do I know ? he thought. Half-frightened, shameful things. It's fine that you finally came, she had said. That such a thing had been said to him by a woman like that, *that* was fine. An enchantment from something unknown. Not from Gudrun, it was something else. He had to look out the window a while in order to become calm again and let the enchantment sink down inside him.

His thoughts were interrupted by some unexpected words from Grete:

'Will you help me a little, Olaf ?'

He looked quickly over at the sleeping midwife.

'No, it's nothing I want,' Grete said quickly and softly. 'It's something else. Would you help me just a little?'

'Yes,' he promised blindly, without thinking that it might conflict with everything else he had already promised.

'What do you want me to do?'

'I just lie here and it's all so wonderful,' she said, 'but I'm quite aware that it hasn't had as great an effect on everyone. I'm thinking especially about this little tike's father.'

Tall, hard Karl; was it he?

'Karl?'

She nodded.

'Karl has an awful hard time of it now and then – and you've been told the reason for that, too.'

'Yes.'

'But I wonder if it's not going to be better for him, now that he's created a little tike like this, after all that misery?'

When she said it, it sounded so probable and sure.

'Do you know where your sister has put him tonight?'

'Up in the attic. They're both there.'

'No, you said the other one had gone out.'

'Yes.'

'But now, won't you go up to Karl?'

'Now?'

'Yes, right away. It's an extra good time now that the other one is outside.'

'What'll I do there?'

It was difficult for her to explain.

'Just see if he's there – well, I mean – of course, he's there. But maybe there's something – '

She stopped. There was something she did not want to say.

'It's not so easy for Karl,' she finally said.

'No,' he answered, without knowing why.

'And you've already promised, you know, so it's too late to back out. I'm stubborn that way, when someone's already promised to do an errand for me.'

'Then tell me what I should do up there.'

'That's why I called you, too,' she told him. 'I just called a tiny bit when I heard you pass in front of the door, and it was fine you came in.'

Oh, he thought, that was the sound I heard.

'But what should you do?' she continued, and it did not sound particularly pleasant: 'Just go up and sit with Karl a while.'

Olaf looked at the sleeping midwife.

'Are you sure she's asleep?'

'Why do you ask that? She has no reason to pretend for us.'

'Well – what shall I say to him?'

'Just go up and keep him company. He's not asleep. Then you'll see. The rest will take care of itself, according to what Karl wants. I'm sure he'll talk to you.'

'I don't understand any of this,' said Olaf as he stood up.

'No, but please go on now. If he asks about me – well, you've seen how I am.'

They were finished whispering. Olaf was ready to leave. Her hand held him back a moment.

'What is it?' he asked, tensed.

'No – just that – I *know* they're having a hard time of it and still I just lie here enjoying myself. And I want it that way! But you'll never be able to understand the least bit of that.'

'You go to sleep now,' he dared to say, in a special way she surely understood.

'Go on now.'

'Is he waiting for me?'

She smiled.

'Are you scared? No, he's not waiting for you. Are you going right up to Karl now?'

'Yes.'

He left, with her happiness tingling inside him.

20

$\cdot$THERE WAS NO ONE in the living room when Olaf looked in. Sissel was not there. She must still have been sleeping on the chair in the kitchen. Olaf did not check. But he stood in the hall a while before he went up the stairs.

What if the thumping sounds through the house now? But it was quiet.

The stairs creaked. Not even he, who knew them so well, could make them be silent. In the daytime no noise could be heard.

Karl can hear steps now –

The attic was, as usual, full of junk. It was divided in two by a partition with a door in the middle of it. In the inner part there was room for beds. No light was turned on up there, nor did Olaf reach for the switch – it was enough with the light that came in through the large window in the gable.

The door to the inner room was open and Karl's voice sounded out gruffly:

'Who's that?'

'Me,' answered Olaf without thinking, since this was his own house. 'Olaf,' he added afterwards.

Karl mumbled something back.

Olaf went in anyway. It was a pretty poor guest room Sissel had fixed up. Some blankets on a discarded iron bed and on an equally discarded divan.

Karl was fully dressed and sat in a chair that was there. He had taken his jacket off in the warm weather.

'Well?' he said sharply. 'What's going on?'

'Nothing.'

Karl stood up quickly.

'I just asked what was the matter,' he said threateningly. 'Don't go telling me that you came up here for your own pleasure.'

Olaf said quickly:

'I was sent up, but there's nothing the matter.'

'Who sent you?'

'Grete.'

'What – '

'Nothing! She's fine.'

Olaf's voice was unsteady. Karl did not look especially kind *now*.

'But she sent you up to me? Just now?'

'Yes, sure. She said you weren't asleep.'

'But what about you – do you usually wander around in the middle of the night?'

'Not when I have any place to sleep,' answered Olaf a bit testily.

'Oh, yes, that's right. I'm sorry,' said Karl with a short smile.

'Are you afraid of something tonight?' Karl continued. 'You almost look like it.'

'No, not much.'

Olaf tried to answer calmly. He actually was quite afraid of Karl. Karl stared at him and finally asked:

'Just who do you think you are, anyway?'

'What do you mean?'

'I've got a right to ask you that after the way you behaved downstairs this evening.'

'I had promised to stand by her.'

'I thought as much. They both struggle to get help for themselves. It's not so easy to have them around constantly, let me tell you.'

Olaf said nothing. Karl continued:

'You saw how I behaved this evening.'

'Yes.'

'I get that way often,' said Karl.

'Yes – '

Suddenly Karl shifted to something else.

'What has Gudrun told you about me?'

Olaf jumped.

'Nothing much.'

'I know what she's told you. But that doesn't make any difference.

We'll not talk about that! And now Grete has had a baby. Let's go down to her, Olaf,' he said impulsively, but reconsidered: 'Oh, no – she ought to try to get some sleep.'

'What should I do up here ?' asked Olaf. 'I don't get the idea.'

'Oh, she tries all sorts of things – '

Olaf was not afraid any longer. Karl continued:

'Maybe she'll succeed sometime. Right now she's very powerful, let me tell you.'

Karl sat calmly and spoke softly – he who only a short while before had shouted and thrown. Olaf stood up.

'Are you going ?'

'Yes, there doesn't seem to – '

'You can just as well stay a while. I don't feel so good at night.'

Olaf stopped. Karl almost looked as if he, too, was going to demand a promise, but it came to nothing, other things intruded: the stairs began creaking again. They both heard it. Careful, stealthy steps that did not tell who it might be.

The door opened in the outer room. They sat quietly, could not see the door from where they sat.

Then a question came, like a breath of air:

'Are you up here, Olaf ?'

Sissel.

Karl started and looked around quickly. Olaf also started. What in the world ? Neither of them answered. Olaf meant to answer, but for some reason could not.

She came toward them in the shimmering light. Knew her way around in the attic and did not stumble over the boxes and scrap lying in her path. Olaf grew warm as he sat there.

Then Sissel was standing in the doorway. Filled it with youth in the gentle half-light.

'Are you here, Olaf ?'

Karl was sitting so that he hid Olaf from her. She saw only Karl. Karl stood up.

'Yes, Olaf's here,' he said dully. 'He's sitting in back of me here.'

Sissel stood still. Was she blushing or wasn't she? The light could not be trusted.

'I – I beg your pardon,' she stammered, facing Karl. 'I thought that he might be here.'

'Well, what do you want?' Olaf finally got out, in order to help her.

'I've got to talk to you,' she answered.

Sissel was not her usual easy-going and intrepid self. She stood there and her face flamed. Olaf felt troubled by it.

Karl was tall and imposing in the low attic room.

'Don't you have any place to sleep, either, because of us? I'm awfully sorry.'

'That makes no difference,' she replied quickly. She stared entranced at Karl.

'Well, what do you want?' repeated Olaf.

She snapped out of it and answered:

'I heard you come up here – and I've got to talk with you right away.'

As she spoke she continued to stare entranced at Karl. Could not help herself. Karl just stood there large and dark.

'Yes, I was sent up here,' said Olaf, desperately trying to fill the dangerously empty seconds.

'Oh? Well, are you finished? Can you come down now?'

'Yes, soon,' he answered. 'You just go ahead.'

Karl remained standing there as before; it was he who had the authority in the room. But there was also something helpless about him as he turned to Sissel:

'Are you going?'

'Guess I'd better,' she answered nervously.

'Thanks for coming up,' he said.

Sissel stared at him.

'I guess you'd better go, then,' he continued.

'Yes – ' she just breathed out.

She walked backward toward the door. Olaf wanted to follow her, but Karl grasped his shoulder.

'Sometimes I need to ask for help. Just a little help. She knew that when she sent you up here. But I don't need it tonight. Tonight I'm strong.'

Olaf did not understand what he was talking about. He thought about how Karl, who had been injured in the war, had broken a footstool earlier in the evening and had that harsh tone in his voice. Karl took his hand away and said:

'Go on now. Thanks a lot.'

Olaf looked quickly at Sissel who was still standing there wrought-up and not herself, but still lovely and soft in that light, and ashamed of something. He shoved her out the door and toward the stairs. They did not know what Karl was doing, they heard no sound.

'That was strange,' said Olaf when they were standing down in the hall.

'What was strange?'

'Oh, I don't know.'

'Well, then I'd just be quiet if I were you!' she said, angry and on the point of tears. 'Just shut up, too! Fool!'

He was about to give it right back to her – but then he remembered that Gudrun was lying nearby. In his own room. The only room he had not yet been in. The only one he had not visited was Gudrun.

'Pretty soon I'll have been in all the rooms – '

'What?' asked Sissel, confused – she had heard his unusual tone of voice.

'There's just one left now.'

'Oh?'

Sissel still had not caught on.

'My own.'

He could not go in there. He wanted to go in as on a carpet of tension and fright and hidden joy to see if Gudrun were sleeping. Then he would have left again.

'Shall we peek in?' asked Sissel, glad to be able to seize it.

93

'No.'

'You can if you want to.'

A shock went through him. What was it she was tempting him with? It gave him strength, a gift from her. Sissel saw immediately that she had won and continued calmly:

'Let's peek in and see if she's sleeping. Since it's been such a hectic evening.'

They were right beside the door, all they had to do was stretch out an arm. Sissel stretched her arm out.

'No – ' said Olaf, but not in time, Sissel had opened the door a crack. No lamp was lit on the night table and all was still. Sissel closed the door noiselessly.

'She must be sleeping. Well, what'll we do? We've no place to sleep, you and I.'

Sissel spoke softly, but still was nervous and wrought-up and unrecognizable.

'Well, what would *you* have done?' Olaf asked.

'Don't look at me like that!'

'Why don't you go for a walk?' he said.

'That's a good idea,' she answered listlessly. 'There's someone down by the old car,' she added and looked out the hall window.

'Yes, it's that flutterer digging in the car.'

'Come on in, Olaf,' said a voice in the room through a crack in the door. In order to avoid making noise, Sissel had not shut the door tightly.

'Listen – ' said Sissel. Then she turned on her heel and walked quickly and restlessly out into the yard. Just sort of out! Olaf, filled by the call, saw how she just set out into the warm night. She did not go down the driveway in the direction of the man and the car. But in another direction. Toward no one.

21

HE STOOD THERE filled by the call.

So he could go into that room after all.

Now the way was clear.

He tried to change somehow inside himself. And succeeded.

'Aren't you there any longer?' asked the voice inside the room.

The way was clear. He carefully pushed the door to his own bedroom open. Caught sight of Gudrun's head on the pillow. On the chair by the bed lay her clothes neatly folded.

She did not move. Just blinked with her eyes for him to come nearer. Her eyes and brow showed above the edge of the blanket. And the unruly lock of hair.

'I heard you talking with someone. Anything wrong?'

'No, not much.'

'Wasn't it something about us?' she asked. 'That's what I thought right away. That something new had happened.'

'Is everyone all right?' she continued when he did not answer.

'Yes, everything's just like when you went to bed.'

He was waiting for something else.

'Can you tell that this is my room?'

'I knew that before. Why don't you sit down. Take my clothes and put them somewhere else. But just don't sit on them.'

He picked up the pile of clothes. Set them down. Strange. He sat down on the chair right beside her head. There lay Gudrun. She had become real. It was too dark, he thought.

'Can I turn the light on.'

She nodded. The light came on and he could see her better. Her dark eyes had been wide open, now they closed themselves quickly. The room was filled with the scent of the clean sheets Sissel had put on the bed.

'Comfortable?'

The lock of hair bobbed up and down.

If she thumps on the floor now, I won't go *right* away, he thought. The thumping he now heard came from his own heart. He was also sure he could have heard Gudrun's heart thumping through all the layers on top of it, but he did not dare lean over. Did she know what he knew? Maybe much more? Would she say anything about it?

'Why did you call?' he asked with a thumping joy inside him.

'Wanted to find out if you'd seen Dad.'

'Yes, he's down in the driveway picking at the car.'

'Yes, he's all in a dither now,' said Gudrun. 'But you should have seen him this past year!'

'Oh?'

'Yes, then you'd understand that I told you the truth about him.' It appeared that she did not want to explain more in detail.

'Are all the others inside?'

'All the others are just where they were before,' he said, in order to be finished with the examination. He would not let them come and ruin *this*. The almost imperceptible scent of Sissel's newly-ironed sheets – and their soft rising and falling as Gudrun breathed. Could he stay longer?

'Do you want me to go now?'

She shook her head.

'No.'

'There's been a Gudrun in this house before,' he said in gratitude, and drew near to his secrets.

'Oh?' she said skeptically. 'Must have been a cat or something, then.'

He nodded that that was it. Laughed joyously to himself. All was still. Outside it was a shade lighter already, it must have been past midnight. But it was still a long time until morning. If only Gudrun would take her arms out from under the blanket – he wanted so much to see a little more of her.

'Well, it's a long time until morning yet,' he said. 'Do you want to sleep?'

'Oh – ' she answered indifferently.

He took it as permission to remain sitting, and settled himself a bit more comfortably on the chair.

'I can just as well sit here a bit longer,' he said.

It became still better to be there.

He became braver since Gudrun wanted him to stay. He had to think up something.

'They say I have long arms,' he said and stretched out an arm. 'Do you ?'

'What ?'

'Have long arms ?'

'Want to see ?'

How quickly she understood! That's the way it should be.

She took her right arm out from under the blanket. The arm was bare and lovely. He looked at it.

'Hmm – ' he said.

A little later he said:

'Shall we see whose is longest ?'

'Sure, why not ?'

She extended her lovely arm toward him. Olaf's shirtsleeves were already turned up and he pushed one the rest of the way up to his shoulder – and then they measured. They put their arms together and placed their fingertips against each other's shoulders. It was strange. This is something big, thought Olaf. They forgot to decide whose arm was longest.

They could do no more. They were speechless and serious. It was quickly over.

'Put it under the blanket again,' said Olaf – for he felt he had to say that, no matter how little he wished it.

'It's not cold,' she answered.

'No, not at all. It's warm enough to go naked, for that matter,' he stammered out.

Gudrun brought her left arm out, too. Olaf saw that the two arms were unceasingly beautiful. He did not try to touch them. Neither of them mentioned anything about seeing more.

He said:

'Now I know that you have fine arms, Gudrun. The finest I've seen.'

Then he said:

'That's strange, too.'

Gudrun still did not answer, and so he asked her a direct question:

'Had you thought it could be so strange?'

Gudrun smiled and answered:

'Never thought about it.'

He didn't believe her. Sure she had. But that was all right.

'We can measure again,' he said.

They did it once more, and it was even almost stranger than the first time. They read something in each other's eyes that they did not dare probe more deeply into. At least, Olaf thought they did.

Olaf mentioned something that was almost frightening:

'Just think how close you were to never coming here! If your car hadn't broken down – '

'Yes, if the car hadn't broken down like that – ' Gudrun began, but then she stopped short and returned to reality:

'Oh, it was terrible in the car. Grete screamed and Dad and the others said the most awful things to each other.'

'We won't talk about that!' Olaf interrupted. 'Or do you really want to?'

'No.'

It faded away. Olaf said instead:

'What do you want to do most of all now?'

'I don't know.'

'Neither do I.'

They stared into space.

Then Olaf thought about the coming morning: all of this would then be gone like a dream and Gudrun would be far away.

It seemed impossible.

'Do you have to leave in the morning?'

'Of course. Karl will get Grete to a hospital somehow. He's good at arranging things like that.'

He looked down at the floor. Gudrun said, unsure of herself:

'You can warm your arm, if you want to.'

'Don't need to,' he said with a heavy heart and rolled his sleeves down. 'It's so warm here that – ' he added.

Then she also hid her lovely round arms under the blanket and said no more.

It was obvious that he had to go now, but it was hard to do it. So senseless. But what else could he do?

'Want to sleep now?'

She nodded and he left. Closed the door after him. He felt a smarting someplace. A faint fragrance hung in the air around him.

22

AND NOW I'VE GOT to find Sissel, he thought.

Why?

Just had to find her. After that. Just see her again as soon as possible.

He listened for a signal from the closed room. Nothing. Sissel was outside, but she was certainly not far away and it should be all right if he left the house. He went out.

It was past midnight, in the first fragile moments of a new day. The dusk of the spring night had only been a pale film over the countryside – now that also was about to disappear. Everything was wrapped in the softness of night, yet was clearly visible.

The sky was overclouded and light, so there were no stars to be seen. But still, it was a starry night, he thought.

A strong scent of flowers rested over the earth. From flowers and herbs that could not be seen individually. The fragrance in the air around Gudrun could not compete with this, which was like the smell of spices from thousands of unknown sources.

Olaf shook himself.

Sissel had run out into this, with tears in her throat. He was sure of that.

Down in the driveway beside the old car someone was scurrying around: one moment crawling under the car, the next moment creeping into it. Fluttering. Olaf turned away. Sissel was surely not down there.

The hill sloped gracefully down to all sides from the house on its top. But in back of the house the slope was not so tidy. A ways down there was a small mound and some bushes. Farther down it gradually blended into the forest. Below the mound was one of Sissel's old hiding places – he was sure to find her there.

He went down there. The bushes and the short, thick grass were wet after the rain, and slept peacefully. There was less dew than usual because of the overclouded sky. Olaf stopped suddenly and stood still. He opened his mouth, but said nothing.

Sissel was there. A warm and good and strange feeling shot through him at the moment he saw her; my sister!

She was as still as the bushes and the grass, was almost part of them. It was warm enough for her to lie there like that. Her face was turned away and she did not see him.

A voice inside him said, no louder than when a raindrop strikes a blade of grass: What's the matter with you –

He had a lump in his throat. The tiny grove was as still as it could possibly be, with its spices and grass, and Sissel bathed herself in it, alone and sick at heart.

He could not move.

He called to her:

'Sissel – '

She started, and jumped up bursting with tension, headed straight for him, snatching up her blouse as she came. But he still saw how beautiful she was, and the thought surged through him that no one must harm her in any way. But now she was wrought-up and beside herself:

'What are you doing here!' she shouted and sort of swept him away, then retreated into herself and her troubles again. He himself was moved and troubled by it, and left quickly.

When she was out of sight behind the small mound, he stopped. The night was blue and still.

A strange shock streaked through him:

All that I'm going to learn and feel!

The light spring night became friendly around him at the thought.

23

OLAF DID NOT GO UP to the yard right away. He just wandered around a bit, filled with his thoughts, dragged his feet through the wet grass, looked down at the grass – and then he ran into a tree. The first birch at the edge of the forest. And a short distance away stood Tore.

There was Tore. Just like that. Like out of a dream.

They stared at each other.

'Are you still here?' asked Olaf sharply.

Not even the sharpest tone of voice could scratch Tore now.

'Sure. Still here – ' he replied. 'That's all right, isn't it?'

He looked around at all the birch trunks and smiled happily – although he was a pretty sorry sight. His shoes were wet, his clothes soaking and disheveled. But it was easy to see that it made no difference to him at the moment.

He nodded to Olaf:

'I'm down here now, but in the morning I'll come up to the house.'

He said it with both authority and uncertainty at the same time and Olaf understood it and approved of it. The sharp reluctance he had felt at first now gave way to a spark which flew between them: understanding. Something fine they had seen and knew about. Tore became a companion. Now we both have a girl, Olaf thought secretly far far inside.

Tore said:

'If you think I'm crazy for wandering around here tonight and not going to bed – well, you can just think so, for all I care. I *am* a bit crazy.'

He just stood there and his voice sounded between the birch trunks. He was a good companion.

'And in the morning I want to see Sissel.'

'Shall I *tell* her that? That you're coming?'

'Sure. Might as well.'

They walked along a bit farther. With tremulous heart Olaf had jumped across the difference in years and was walking between the same trees and thinking about the same things as Tore.

They walked along a bit farther. Then Tore turned off.

'Be seeing you,' he said unceremoniously.

'I just can't sleep tonight,' he continued frankly, and disappeared into the dim forest, wet through from the rain, happy. Early in the morning he would reappear.

24

THE YARD WAS EMPTY. Down at the turn of the driveway the man was still working on the car. Olaf went quickly into the house, he had to find Sissel. She was in the living room, refreshed by her bath in the warm spring night.

'What are you doing roaming around all the time?' she asked.

Her tone of voice was belligerent, but he paid little attention to that.

'I've just been talking to Tore,' he said.

'Tore? Now?'

'Yes, he was down in the birches.'

They stared at each other. Something fragile and precious was in danger. Olaf groped after it, but could only continue bluntly:

'He said he'd come in the morning.'

'Who?'

'Tore's coming in the morning.'

Olaf made it sound like something inevitable. He was puzzled and hurt by the change that had come over her.

She tossed her head briskly and said:

'That's all right by me.'

Then she left. Where was it now, that delicate and nameless something? He said sternly at her disappearing back:

'You can go in with Grete. They're awake in there now. I can hear them.'

Sissel stopped.

'Why?'

'You can just go in there, I said! You've got to be someplace!'

She gave in and went toward Grete's door. Knocked softly, and went in.

Olaf did not have long to wonder about what he would do now that he had no bed to sleep in – for now the thumping he was waiting for finally came. Since he had been waiting nervously for it, he started violently.

But he felt it almost as a relief that it finally had come. He went out into the hall and into her room immediately.

The room was the same as it had been earlier, except that a steadily increasing morning mood now filled it. The woman in Sissel's bed was, however, not the same. She looked at him desperately:

'He isn't coming!' she said without further introduction. 'That's Olaf, isn't it?'

'Do you want me to leave?' he asked.

'Come here.'

He saw that she was frightened.

'Have you seen Hjalmar?'

'Yes. He's down in the driveway.'

'In the driveway? Oh, how I wish he would come up here! I've got something important to tell him.'

'He's down there fixing the car,' Olaf said nervously. She saw immediately what was going on inside him and asked in that whispering tone of voice they had to use, they who must not be heard:

'Are you afraid of me, too?'

'No, but – '

'You have no reason to be afraid, either. It's worse for Hjalmar and me. I can't stand him – you can't imagine how little of him I can stand – and so the most awful things happen. Sit down, this will take a while – I'm so afraid he *won't* come tonight. It's somehow now that he has to come.'

Olaf sat down. It was terrible how different it all was from room to room: in this room there was only naked need.

'Then he gets so furious at what I say that he wishes misfortunes on me – and then I feel that I just have to see to it that he gets his wish. *I can't help myself.* Just think of it!'

'Yes, you told me that before,' Olaf stammered out. It was not easy for him to be mixed up in it.

'I just couldn't speak to him after he had wished I was dumb – but that's not the worst of it, there are other things bothering me more. And tonight, now that I can't talk either, they're bothering me ten times as much.'

Olaf did not know what to do or say. In order to do something, he took her ring out of his pocket and laid it on the night table.

'Here's your ring.'

'What do you mean?' she asked suspiciously.

'I was supposed to help you if any of the others tried to – but none of them want to hurt anyone!'

'Did I say they did? Oh, well, I thought it, anyway. But I've been lying here a long time since then. I just wish that he felt that he had to come to me here. Just think how he's carried me! That's what it is.'

'Oh?'

'It's an awful thing to have made yourself dumb,' she said.

Olaf dared to ask her:

'Would it do any good if I called to him and asked him to come up here now?'

She quickly made herself hard.

'No, don't! I'm not going to send for him so soon after he wished me dumb. He can come by himself. And don't go sneaking off to get him, either! I'll be able to see it on him if you do.'

Olaf was staring into a maze with no exit. He tried to collect his scattered thoughts. Everything was blocked as by a wall.

'But the way he's carried me – ' she began again, angry at herself.

'Well, when a person's lame – ' he began.

'Yes, but what if I wasn't *that*, either?'

He grew tense inside.

'And he's been carrying me ever since,' she continued. 'That puny little thing has almost killed himself carrying me. Over a year now.'

'It's not true!' said Olaf numbly.

'But it is true. I've never even tried to walk since he said it. He's not been away from me a single day since.'

She stopped – as if she were waiting for Olaf to say something, but he only looked uncomprehendingly at her.

'He wished that on me at the hardest moment we've ever had together. What it was we were arguing about makes no difference now. And ever since, he's carried. He's never gotten tired.'

She was, at any rate, not angry at him now; that was easy to hear. In the morning he'd come and it would all be over, Olaf thought.

'It's getting closer and closer,' she said and continued from where she had left off.

'Yes – ' was all Olaf could say.

'I'm afraid of him when he isn't here!'

'But shouldn't I try to get him?' asked Olaf once more.

She shook her head.

'He'll come when he's ready. It's no use before.'

'What?'

'But that's why I called you,' she admitted. 'To find out where he was. For it's getting closer in here now!'

She said that last as if she were not getting enough air.

'What was he like when you last saw him?' she asked.

'He said he would come.'

'Said he would come! What good does that do? He just says and says. We've got to plan something. I'm so afraid he won't come – '

She listened. Just then a thump sounded in the silence. Perhaps it was only Karl in the attic moving a chair. But she jumped so that she struck her head on the headboard and asked wildly:

'What was that?'

'Nothing.'

'Look out the window. Do you see anything?'

'There's nothing out there,' answered Olaf, but looked out the window just the same. The shade was not drawn and the window faced the night-still forest.

'Nothing.'

'I guess I'm just too jumpy,' she said and got her breath back. 'That's the way it is when you lie waiting for something that isn't good! Listen now, they're not on my side, none of the others, I haven't done anything to deserve that. But he's just carried and carried! We've got to plan something,' she said excitedly.

'I can't!'

'What can you do, then?' she asked in desperation. 'Go get him for me, then!' she said and gave in to him. 'No matter what – just get him. He's carried too long. He knows I can walk! Get him!'

She had hold of Olaf. Now she took her hand away so that he could go.

'If I can,' he stammered out.

'If he will, you mean,' she said, frightened, and listened into the stillness.

'I'm listening for sounds,' she told him. 'Every single sound somehow means danger for me. Do you hear anyone coming?' she asked nervously.

It was as still as it could possibly be.

'Well, then go. But be sure to bring him back! You don't know how he's tried to make it up to me.'

'I'm going – '

'He's funny, too,' she said gently and stumbled onto a faint and long-forgotten lover's lane.

Olaf hurried out.

25

THE LIVING ROOM WAS STILL EMPTY when Olaf looked in. Sissel must have been in with Grete. Up in the attic slow steps moved back and forth. That would be Karl. The room he was in was directly over the hall. It was small, and Karl turned and walked back.

Olaf went out into the yard to look for Hjalmar. He now had a new picture of him. Once out in the yard, Olaf had to look up at the yellow wall of the house – in wonder that it still looked the same – now that every one of its rooms was occupied by unexpected strangers. He almost believed that he could have felt it vibrating if he had touched it. An incredible night. From every room came calls to him, and he had to go in.

The man to be summoned was not to be seen down by the car. But he was undoubtedly fluttering around somewhere in the vicinity and would be easy to find. How should Olaf go about delivering his important message? He understood well enough that it was important, he was excited and happy to have been given the opportunity to deliver it. If only he could have just called down: Come in, come in! There was something like that about it.

He looked a bit absent-mindedly at the meadow mist which was drifting across the hill.

But he was given no time for reflection, for suddenly the old car began to thunder and rattle. The motor chugged and sprang to life, and the noise increased.

Olaf stood rooted to the spot. Hjalmar must have gotten it started somehow!

The racket increased. But the sound of the motor was certainly not as it should have been. Olaf had been around cars enough to hear that there was something seriously wrong with it. What had he done to it? – But at least he had gotten it started.

The car suddenly gave a jerk and came charging and rattling up the hill.

The noise seemed to fill completely the quiet night, and jangled meaninglessly in Olaf's ears. It did not seem right that the car had come to life and was moving up the hill, it was big and black and eerie, it was dead – but was moving toward him.

Olaf did not know why he did it – he probably wanted to warn the others – at any rate he ran quickly into the house and into the living room. But the car had already sent out a warning: Sissel came running out of Grete's room and over to him, over to the window, and cried out:

'What's gotten into the car!'

'Just started going, all by itself.'

He knew very well that a man was sitting in it, but still it somehow came by itself, noisily, bent on running the house down. Aimed straight at the house, with an eerie, slow, dragging speed.

'Can it be that flutterer?'

'He's been working at it a long time now.'

'But can he drive?'

'You can see perfectly well that he can't!'

Olaf and Sissel had run to the window. Now steps came running down the stairs, Karl came into the room.

'You've heard it, too!'

Sissel jumped, as if she wanted to hide, but could not. Olaf noticed it and reached over and touched her: his sister filled with a feeling of shame toward Karl and the coming meeting with Tore - and everything. It was good to touch her now – as friend and companion. As the car came up the hill.

'Will you look at that!' said Karl. 'How did that happen?'

'He's been down there a long time.'

'Yes, and now there's going to be an accident,' Karl said, and the darkness before the accident quickly fell about them.

'Why?'

Olaf shouted that out. As if in protest. A hasty protest against accidents. Karl answered:

'Can't you see that he can't drive?'

'But he got it started!' Sissel said defiantly. An unnecessary defiance. They were all speaking in breathless haste as the car approached.

'Do you call that getting it started?' retorted Karl, unnecessarily sharply, and ran out as if to take the coming shock. The racket had wakened others. The midwife peeked out of Grete's door and Grete's voice could be heard in back of her:

'What's Karl doing?'

'Nothing!' Olaf called back. 'He just went out.'

Was there a thumping coming from Kristine's room? No. There was too much happening all at once. Hasn't Gudrun come? Everything was whirling around. They stood nailed to the spot and watched as the car approached, and listened as the broken-down motor labored. Olaf called out:

E

'He can't turn it, and he can't stop! He'll hit the house!'

'Watch out!' he shouted to Sissel, but they could not move. Just waited for the crash.

Now –

The car kept coming straight up the hill and in their fright it appeared to be larger than the house. It had picked up speed on the flat at the top of the hill and it now moved forward quickly, somber and carrying Death. But Karl was there. Sissel and Olaf watched as Karl made a frantic jump at the passing running-board and managed to hang on. The man inside the car had fortunately rolled the window down with his nervous hands – Karl reached in through the opening, grabbed the wheel and swung the car enough so that it did not crash into the wall with its full weight. The impact came at an angle, the bumper and fender glanced off the house. But there was still a rending crash that shook the frame house to its foundations, a ripping along the clapboard – and as the house gave under the shock a dim haze descended over the sight and thoughts of the onlookers, confused everything for half a second – then their sight and thoughts cleared again.

Then they saw Karl and his father thrown forward. The father against the windshield, Karl more to the side as he still stood on the running-board with one arm reaching into the car. Karl had also gotten hold of the brake, so that the car stopped after the crash and scraped only a short ways along the wall – with a tearing sound to those inside the house. Then everything stood still. Karl and his father got hold of themselves and got to their feet and out of the car, a bit cut up from bits of broken glass, but otherwise uninjured.

Olaf and Sissel got their breath back.

Through the open door sounded Grete's voice again:

'What's Karl doing?'

The midwife turned and said breathlessly that everything was all right. Sissel ran toward the door, shouting wildly:

'He did it! He jumped on the running-board – '

Gudrun came running down the hall in a long armless nightgown, ran to the window and looked out at the car and the two men. She asked out loud:

'Was it Dad again?'

No one answered in the confusion. Olaf looked stealthily at her.

'I know it was Dad,' she said. 'That's the sort of thing he's always doing.'

'But he really is nice,' she continued tenaciously.

'Oh dear, they've cut themselves,' said Sissel, and that released them: they all three ran out to the men. The driver's brow was bleeding and Karl was cut on the chin. One of the arms of Karl's jacket was torn, but his arm was not injured. They stood shaking their heads, trying to clear their minds, bleeding slightly.

'It's nothing,' said Karl when the three came up. 'Just a scratch. We're all right. Leave us alone,' he said irritably, although no one had made a move to touch him. Gudrun hovered around her father:

'Are you hurt?'

'No, no,' he said, his face shining. 'Not at all. I sure handled that fine, didn't I?' He pushed Gudrun aside, wiped his face, had eyes only for the car, felt the tires, lifted the hood, looked at the damage on the left side, laughed a little, fluttered, as if carried away by it all.

'Stop that!' Karl said sharply. They noticed each other for the first time and began an excited conversation.

'Just what did you think you were doing, anyway?'

The father was filled to overflowing by what had happened.

'It almost ran right into the house – ' he said and looked in fright at the splintered yellow wall. 'Right at the house – and faster and faster! Went just like a shot right at the house!'

'Yes, but what did you do down there?' asked Karl. 'How did it get started?'

'I just pulled at all those things, over and over again – and all of a sudden it started going. My God! now I've driven a car, too – '

'And so you thought you'd run the house down?'

It did not appear that Karl could calm himself down so quickly.

'No, no – run the house down – '

'But you can't run a house down. You just kill yourself! That's what you nearly did.'

The other man just rocked his head in amazement:

'Straight at the house. I just pulled something down there and it started going – '

He began digging in the pile of metal again. Karl took hold of him and pushed him away from the car as if he were a piece of fluff.

'Just you stay away. We'll have no more of your tricks.'

The father fell. Gudrun let out a frightened cry. Then she looked quickly over at Olaf who had seen it all and who stood there shocked by it. She took a step toward him and said compellingly:

'But they really are nice.'

She caught his eye, so that they could together raise the two men up – and for her sake he unhesitatingly took part in it.

Her father quickly scrambled to his feet; he was insulted and enraged:

'Which one of us was it that got the car going, anyway? That fixed it? It wasn't you. You just sat down there and shouted and carried on when it stopped last night! It didn't help any what you pulled at. But just look here, I'll get it – '

Karl grabbed him again and held him tight. Sissel and Olaf looked questioningly at each other and could not understand Karl's anger now that it was all over and had turned out so well. He must still have been a bit shaken up after the collision.

'Don't you know what I have in that house?' he shouted in the same wild tone of voice they had heard him use before. Then he got hold of himself, turned toward Sissel and Olaf with a concerned look on his face and said with an embarrassed shrug:

'I'm sorry. I was only thinking about my own – '

They looked back at him in concern.

The father waved his arms:

'You don't understand anything about it. I got the car started right away.'

'Well, you can just leave it alone after this!' said Karl gruffly. 'Or you'll end by killing us all.'

112

Gudrun forced her way between Sissel and Olaf in her light blue nightgown, looked at them anxiously and repeated the words she never grew tired of saying:

'There was no one as nice as Karl,' she said softly.

Only Sissel and Olaf heard it.

In the house they heard Grete's voice:

'Karl! Come in here.'

His shouting must have been heard in there, too.

He raised his head.

'All right. I'm coming,' he answered, but did not have the strength to tear himself free and go in immediately. He stood there plagued by anger, regret and his own shouting. The air was still full of that shouting. The father muddled around and tried to make himself heard. Only his shut-in wife sent no signal. Olaf was a bit surprised that she did not thump, but she must have been waiting expectantly for her husband to come. Olaf remembered *that*, now that the excitement had died down, but there was obviously no use giving the man the message yet – he had thoughts only for his driving skill and purred and chattered about it. In a little while –

'Listen here now,' he said and straightened up and wiped a few drops of blood from his brow. 'Doesn't make the least bit of difference what you say, Karl; it was me who got it started. You can't explain that away if you explain yourself blue in the face. I drove up the hill. Right straight at the house. But just in the nick of time I turned – '

Karl kept quiet. His father was elated:

'My God! the way it started chugging and moving! I just wish Kristine could have seen it. But nobody was around to see and hear it all.'

Olaf stepped forward and began clearing his throat. For now the man had mentioned Kristine, so maybe it was a good moment to –

'What do you want?' Karl said suddenly and belligerently to him.

Olaf jumped back as if he had been caught doing something wrong. It would just have to wait. He crowded close up to Sissel who was standing looking defiantly at Karl. Then Gudrun laid her hand on his arm, and he thought she looked so wonderful standing there in her nightgown that he went along with her in accepting Karl.

'You cold?' he asked her unnoticed by the others.

'Cold? No!'

No, that was right. It was a night when girls lay stock still in the grass, he thought, and liked feeling Sissel standing close beside him. How warm it was!

It was Karl who had the right to work on the car. It now appeared that he was busy trying to get the motor started again. His face still bore a threatening expression. The children were still young enough to be interested in finding out if he could get it started, and so they remained standing there. And suddenly the machine started. They jumped at the sound. Karl immediately shut it off again. But now it was all right. The man who had just driven it had not calmed down yet. He touched his brow, where the wound no longer bled:

'Doesn't make any difference. Just all a lot of fun. From now on I'm going to do the driving! Come here, boy,' he suddenly said to Olaf. 'I can talk to you about driving. Say – will you just look at Gudrun!' he exclaimed proudly. 'Isn't she something? She sure makes you sit up and take notice – '

Olaf felt a shock run through him. Gudrun stared into space. They were all worried about Hjalmar's behavior. Karl pulled angrily at the damaged fender and ripped it free. A call came from the house.

'Karl!'

He did not hear and Sissel stepped forward. Olaf watched the redness once more rising in her face under Karl's eyes.

'You'd better go in. She's calling.'

He nodded. Felt something cut through rage and turmoil. Something that softened his expression.

'Go on,' said Sissel with some sort of authority behind her words, 'she's already called a couple of times.'

'All right,' he replied.

114

He went immediately.

Sissel dug with the toe of her shoe in the gravel.

Hjalmar now had the field for himself. He puffed himself up and began bragging about his driving. A cool morning wind blew across the yard and Gudrun ran into the house to get her coat. She returned immediately. Olaf meant to deliver the message from Kristine, but when the man saw his open mouth he started talking a blue streak himself:

'Just wait a minute. Let me talk. I guess it's me who should do the talking around here now.'

He felt the dried blood on his brow and his eyes shone. He kept talking:

'Karl never will learn to drive. He never learns anything decently.'

They listened to him silently. Sissel was ready to leave at any moment. He noticed it and said quickly:

'Don't go! Please don't you go, too.'

Gudrun looked steadily at Olaf and supported her father. There was now not much from keeping him from going under – as he stood there flailing wildly with his ridiculous bragging and nonsense. But Gudrun was supporting him. Olaf did not get a chance to break into a scornful grin. Besides, he was burning with Kristine's message. But it was a secret message, he had decided; he would have to wait until he was alone with the man.

But Hjalmar obviously did not wish to be alone with him. He had turned to Sissel, who was the only adult present, and in effect forced her to remain. He clung to the car door and preached to them.

'You know, that was quite an idea, girl: driving, that is. I've just lost my job and don't have anything to do. What do you think?'

Sissel stood there and listened patiently. That encouraged the man so that he let go of the car door and went up to them. So that they could see his friendly, beautiful eyes, which were ceaselessly searching. It was really easy for Gudrun to support him. She looked compellingly at Olaf. Then she whispered into his ear:

'See him?'

'Yes.'

'Isn't he like I say?'

'Yes, he is.'

Olaf thought:

Otherwise he couldn't have carried like that.

Now I have to talk with him about Kristine.

It hasn't occurred to anyone that she, too, should be told what it was that shook the house, flashed through his mind. Maybe the midwife has told her. Not even Gudrun has thought about that –

How could this man have been so mean to another person as he had been to her in the car? And once before he had wished that she never again would be able to use her feet.

Olaf stared helplessly into a maze.

What if her door had now swung open and she had come walking out! No one could know. She was so sorry for it all that she was nearly beside herself and had wanted to make up for it.

In the middle of these thoughts he turned his attention to the scene before him. The man's voice was still cheerful and saucy. He nodded to Gudrun:

'Hi, there – '

She nodded back at her father.

'But you'd better get some clothes on,' he said. 'Or get back in bed. It's still the middle of the night – this has really been a night,' he reminded himself.

'I've got my coat on now,' replied Gudrun.

'Well, just the same – you might catch cold.'

Then his face broke into a smile over the recent events.

'Now, you see – yes, you, too,' he said to Olaf and Sissel. 'I've just narrowly escaped death. That's why everything's sort of special for me.'

They did not answer. It gripped them too strongly.

116

'Don't you think that's why?'

'Yes, we think so,' answered Sissel quietly.

The man looked toward the house and said:

'I think I'm going to go in to her pretty soon – '

He said that more to himself than to the others, testing – and Olaf grasped the opportunity:

'That's just what she's waiting for – '

'You be quiet about it!' he interrupted. 'What do you know about it? You only scare me by saying things like that. You just make me put it off. Anyway, I haven't told you about the car.'

A stream of words began flowing out of him:

'Now, you see, that lousy car was just about to smack right into the house, but in the last second I turned – '

They could not tell him that it was Karl who had done that and thus saved him. And Gudrun had not even seen what had happened.

'You see, I saw the house rising up in front of me. The house was moving and I stood still – it was all twisted around like that for me. My whole body tightened up and I thought: this is the end. Just the end, if you can understand that. Do you?' he asked Sissel, who was grown-up.

'Yes.'

He was swept along by her answer and beamed at her:

'And so it all turned out fine!'

Gudrun beamed at Olaf.

'And now I'm going in,' he said, carried along by this wave which gave him courage.

'Yes,' said Olaf. 'I was supposed to – '

The man interrupted him:

'Are you trying to scare me away from it? I'm going in now. Now's the time – even if it is the middle of the night.'

He did not go in, but kept fluttering around the car. Olaf would just have to wait.

26

SISSEL BROKE THE SILENCE:

'Yes, it's the middle of the night,' she said suddenly to Gudrun standing beside her. Repeated the words Hjalmar had just used. 'Go to bed now.'

'Why?' asked Gudrun, who was wide awake.

'Because you've been given Olaf's room. So you might as well use it,' Sissel said sharply.

Olaf looked at his sister shocked. Why was she treating Gudrun like that?

Gudrun said, amazed:

'Yes, I know it's his room.'

'Well, then use it. There's nothing to stare at any longer here.'

'He's my dad.'

Olaf felt ashamed. What had gotten into Sissel? The man had heard what had been said and said to Gudrun as he fluttered around:

'Run along now. I'm all right. Just fine.'

Gudrun wrapped her coat tighter around her. Olaf watched. Then she went in.

'Well, now you've had your way,' the man said calmly to Sissel.

'Oh, everything's all messed up tonight!' Sissel burst out.

The man said:

'Yes, I guess it is – '

Olaf glanced accusingly at Sissel. But inside of him a joy sprang up: all messed up tonight? Sure it was all messed up. Wonderfully messed up. And full of flashes of light. Sissel was just overtired and had no place to sleep.

'Well, now I'm going,' said the man.

Olaf had been standing by the house, half filled with what was happening outside, half listening for a signal from inside. But none came. The silence inside the house became gradually heavier. But now the man was going in.

'This isn't easy to do,' he told Olaf. 'And you know that. Where did Karl go?'

'In to Grete,' answered Olaf, who was afraid that it was just another excuse for delaying.

'Someone has to come with me,' the man said.

They saw how tense his face became.

'There's the door,' said Sissel. 'It's easy enough to find.'

She pointed into the hall: '*That* door.'

'*That* door?' he repeated. 'Why do you have to say that? I know very well which door it is. I guess you just don't understand that I'm going in to something difficult. Something I keep putting off. But now that my life has been saved, I'll just go right in and take what's coming to me. Just your standing there makes me nervous,' he ended and waved his arms.

'Excuse me,' said Sissel.

'But somebody has to come with me.'

Sissel shook her head.

'Not you? Well, there you can just see. You won't just up and come with me – never really thought you would, anyway.'

'I don't think you should have anyone with you.'

'Maybe not. You come, then,' he said commandingly to Olaf. 'You've promised to help me. And now there's no way back for me, either.'

Olaf shrunk back.

'But what'll I do in there?'

'Can't I count on you, either? Come on. You're not going back on your promise, are you?'

'Leave Olaf alone,' said Sissel.

Olaf knew how good it would have felt to let Sissel shield him, but he would have to be on his own this time.

'Let me be, Sissel.'

'Sure, he's gone and poked his own nose into this. He started it as soon as we got here,' the man said.

Olaf felt weak inside. Exactly whom should he help, anyway? Just whoever stood before him at the moment, of course.

'This is none of my business,' he said.

But he followed the man into the house and down the hall. Toward the door to that dangerous and silent room – the room that usually was the easiest in the whole house because it was Sissel's.

They said nothing. Olaf was thinking about what he had unwittingly gotten mixed up in. It happened just like that.

The man knocked timidly on the door.

At first they listened for a voice to tell them to come in. But then the man remembered that it was the door to a dumb person – they would just have to go in.

The door opened out and the man pulled it open wide. Then just stood there as if he had opened it for Olaf: he was to go in first.

Olaf had just barely time to think that the man was a coward to send him in first – then he clenched his teeth and stepped into the dark room.

Was it dark in this room?

When Olaf had been there around midnight, it had been light in there, as everywhere else. He started, then realized that the heavy dark shade had been drawn since he had last been there. Had someone been in there, or – ? The midwife must have come in, he decided. Now he could not see anything in the room. Nor hear anything.

The man in back of him whispered:

'You shouldn't have pulled the shade down. She likes to look out into the summer night.'

Olaf had stopped, with his hand on the light switch. But he did not flick it. He was afraid.

'Shall I turn the light on?' he whispered.

'Of course.'

'Wouldn't it be better to let her sleep?'

'You think she's sleeping?' the man said skeptically. 'I know her better than that.'

His arms began to flutter. Unbearably.

'Oh, stop that!' whispered Olaf. He dared for some reason to say such a thing to the older man. The darkness in the room helped.

The man immediately let his arms drop.

All this time the room was silent. Olaf stood with his hand on the light switch, but he did not dare to turn it on. There was nothing living in the room.

How could he know? He just knew somehow.

The man had gotten a grip on himself after his setback, and shoved Olaf.

'Turn the light on. She's not asleep. And you're not getting out of this. You've promised her something against me, so you're going to be here when I make up to her. My God! I can never really make it all up, but – You've got to stay here with me because I'm afraid. Turn the light on, I said.'

Olaf answered numbly:

'Something strange is going on here – '

The man was instantly infected by it. His voice shook:

'What do you mean?'

'Something's wrong here.'

The man turned out to be the braver after all; he turned on the light himself.

Nothing appeared to be wrong. The woman lay with the blankets around her as if she were sleeping. They could see her head and shoulders.

The man said in a quavering voice:

'Everything's all right here.'

'Yes,' agreed Olaf. 'Anyway, she's not lying and watching us.'

Nevertheless, they did not move.

'She's lying there listening,' the man said. 'She has a habit of listening when no one thinks she is.'

'Not now.'

'I'll wake her,' said the man. 'I'll call to her. There's little time to spare now – I've been so terribly mean to her. And she's not asleep. Kristine!' he called, but only half out loud. His voice lost its force at the critical moment.

No answer.

Had she gotten out of bed and drawn the shade? buzzed through Olaf's mind. And this man had carried and carried.

'Kristine! I've driven the car. It was me who crashed into the house. But my life was saved and everything – and I've got to tell you about it. That's why. But there are a lot of other things, too – I've got to tell you that – well, all the other things.'

His voice gradually failed him. There was no movement in the bed.

'Go over there and look,' whispered the man. 'You've promised me just as much as you've promised her.'

Olaf pretended not to hear. He was too young to do that.

'Don't you hear?'

'Yes.'

'Is that the way you keep promises? Please!'

There was no alternative. The man did not dare and there was no time to argue. Olaf started around the bed. He broke into a cold sweat. The man remained standing by the door.

Everything was quiet. Olaf leaned over. Listened for sounds of breathing and knew that there were none. He straightened up and looked imploringly at the man by the door.

'Can come – ' was all he could get out.

'What do you mean by that?'

But the man obeyed, came over, and looked down at the pale face. Then he began waving his arms. Caught himself and stood still again. Then he began digging and rooting around on the night table, among Sissel's things. Found nothing.

Olaf stood there and felt the beads of perspiration on his brow. Not that he saw anything horrible. Her face was just pale and quiet, and only vacant.

'Is she dead?' he whispered.

'No!' said the man and started up violently.

'What are you thinking about?' he said again.

Olaf asked:

'But what are you looking for?'

'Don't know. If she could have taken anything. She doesn't have to be dead just because she's lying still like that. We've got to get hold of a doctor! We've got to get out of here as quick as we can.'

Then he bent over again – under the burden which rested on him. He touched her.

'Dead ? No. Why should she be ?'

Olaf stood silent. The man said:

'But I don't see anything she could have taken. She didn't have anything, either, that I can think of. No, it's something else. A sudden attack.'

'Maybe it was when the car hit the house,' tumbled out of Olaf.

I shouldn't have said that, raced through his mind. The fluttery man became even paler than he already was.

'When I crashed into the house ?'

Olaf said no more.

'So you think that – '

Olaf tried to convince himself that it must have been so. The way she had been lying there afraid of every sound. And in this dark, shut-off room. Was it she who had drawn the shade ?

The man's restless arms hung loosely.

'I don't believe it! And she doesn't have to be dead. But now for a doctor. I've got to tell Karl. Don't touch them,' he ended sternly.

'Don't touch what ?'

'Her eyes.'

Her closed eyes. The man had not dared look at them. He went out of the room. Olaf followed. The man fluttered.

'Thank God the car is fixed, so that we can get it started right away. For it would take longer to send for a doctor – the way it is around here.'

'Yes,' answered Olaf mechanically.

'Well, thank God I fixed the car. Where's Karl ?'

In the living room Sissel got up from the sofa. She must have lain down there again to get a little sleep the rest of the exhausting night.

'What's the matter now ?'

She looked tired.

The man did not stop.

'Something's wrong with Kristine.'

He nodded toward Grete's door:

'Karl's in there, isn't he?'

Sissel nodded.

'Karl, come out here!'

Olaf told Sissel what they had found.

'But have you been in there and drawn the shade?' he asked her.

'No. Why?'

'Nothing.'

Karl came out, angry.

'Can't you ever stop making a racket, Dad? After a while it gets more than – '

'You've got to come out and drive, Karl.'

'Drive?'

'Yes. Kristine's lying in there as if she was dead. Go in and look.'

Karl changed. His annoyance and anger fell off him as if it had been something loosely hung on. His father talked without pause:

'You've got to drive to the doctor. For now the car's fixed. She could have taken something. We don't know anything about her. But the car's fixed now, so – '

Karl did not listen to him very carefully, instead he turned quickly to Olaf.

'Show me where she is. I didn't notice where we carried her. Everything was so mixed up then.'

Olaf hurried out first. It still looked like everything was all mixed up.

'Do you know anything about what happened?' Karl said sternly at Olaf's back.

'No.'

'There's no use hiding anything.'

Olaf felt as if there were a weapon hanging over his head as he walked toward the room.

'We just came in together,' Olaf said unsteadily. 'He said I should come with him. It was dark in here and we turned on the light. We stood still a little while before we could go over to her. She was just lying there as if she was asleep. Like she is now.'

Karl was not satisfied. He stopped:

'But you did something for her yesterday evening. I noticed it.'

Olaf had to stop.

'I didn't do anything,' he answered.

'Oh ?'

'I just promised to help her, because she asked me to.'

'What were you to help her with ?'

'I don't know.'

'All right. Go on.'

Where is Gudrun ? thought Olaf as he walked. He did not dare turn around to see if she was in the living room, but walked ahead with that threat at his back.

'I know very well that she could talk just as good as before, see,' he heard in back of him.

'Yes, but I don't know anything about it!'

'She at least said something to you. Would you please turn around ?'

No one was as nice as Karl – he told himself, and obeyed. He did it mechanically. There was Karl.

'What did she say ?'

'She asked me to help her if she needed it. I think she thought the rest of you were against her.'

Karl nodded.

'Sure. And you took that upon yourself ?'

'Just promised to help her.'

'But you haven't,' said Karl.

'No. I wasn't to come until she signaled for me.'

What *have* I done ? he thought suddenly. But I went every time she thumped and it was for me.

'I came when she knocked,' he mumbled, for now they had entered the room. As he walked over to the bed, Karl said:

'You took something upon yourself you didn't know anything

about and could never have managed. That's why *I* asked you to help *me*, too.'

'What?'

Karl did not answer, he was standing over Kristine. What had Karl asked him to do? Strange. A strange joy over all that was unexpected swept through him at Karl's words. He stored it away. This was no place for joy. But Karl had not been any gun at his back.

Karl stood leaning over the bed. Olaf looked at the black shade. He did not dare mention it. The room was blind.

'Mmm,' said Karl to himself.

Olaf watched as he touched the eyes. Laid the lid gently back again.

'I don't think taking the car is going to help any,' he said. 'But of course we've got to do it.'

His eyes rested on Olaf.

'She's dead, all right.'

It did not surprise Olaf. He was somehow already sure of it.

But Karl's eyes still rested on Olaf. Something else was coming. Karl said:

'Now you've got to try to be nice to my father.'

'Me?' said Olaf almost inaudibly. Now he was surprised.

Karl nodded.

'Because this is going to shake him up more than we can imagine.'

Olaf did not answer.

'Olaf?'

Yes, he was listening and was waiting tensely for what would come next.

Karl said calmly:

'You don't have to worry about the rest of us. Now we all have to help him.'

'Me, too? I'm just a kid,' confessed Olaf and had nothing against admitting it just then.

'Makes no difference,' said Karl. 'It's not a matter of age. But you haven't been in on everything that's made it so hard for the rest of us. We've made it hard for each other, all too often.'

Olaf tried to understand. But what should he do?

'Just be nice to him.'

'All right,' answered Olaf, relieved. Karl looked quickly over at the bed once more and then was finished there.

'Come on, we'd better try to get the car started, like he said. Not that it makes any difference, but – '

They left the room. Olaf wanted to talk about many different things, but could not.

Karl came back to the same thing:

'You see, this won't be easy for him to handle. He'll take it hard.'

'But he's carried and – ' Olaf began, then stopped short.

'Take it easy,' Karl said sharply. He obviously did not want Olaf to mention that.

Olaf hid away still better what he knew about the shade. He was sure that Kristine had drawn it herself.

'What about Gudrun?' occurred to him all of a sudden.

'What about her?'

It was such a wonderful name for him to take into his mouth that he did it again:

'*Gudrun* loves him anyway.'

Karl said:

'We *all* love him. But now remember what I asked you to do.'

Asked you to do, he had said. Big, hard Karl. It affected Olaf deeply, made him feel still more helpless and too young.

27

SISSEL AND THE OLDER MAN came quickly toward them as they entered the living room. Olaf watched Sissel closely: she looked past Karl and looked frightened; no, then she had to shift her eyes over to Karl just the same, quickly, shyly. But she got no response from him.

'Go in there,' Olaf said to her.

'What's the matter with her?'

Olaf did not have to answer, for the fluttering man was buzzing away: 'Are you ready, Karl? We've got to get going. You've got to get the car started. It's your turn this time. My God, we've got to hurry!'

'Take it easy,' said Karl.

'What?'

'She's not alive.'

'And you just stand there and say that. You can't be sure.'

'I'm pretty sure about it. But of course we've got to get a doctor to look at her.'

Sissel was in there now and the midwife came on the run. She had also been told and disappeared into the room.

The man buzzed:

'We've got to leave right away! She may still be alive, even though it doesn't look like it.'

'Yes, yes,' said Karl. 'That's just what we're doing. Where's Gudrun?'

'In her room,' answered Olaf quickly.

'Why can't we use the telephone!' shouted the man. 'I've never seen anything like it. And Gudrun,' he said, 'she doesn't know anything about it yet! Would you go in and tell her, Olaf?'

Olaf was already on the way. He felt how impossible it was to keep the joy and excitement back. Then Karl stuck his head in through the door and stopped him:

'Olaf, come out here and help me with the car a bit.'

'Yes,' interrupted the older man, 'you do that. Before anything else. I'll go in and tell Gudrun myself.'

Olaf was forced to follow Karl out to the car, to help him bend and straighten things that were preventing it from moving. It actually looked like it would be able to go despite its smashed-in front end. The motor began thundering again, filling the light night with its racket. Karl now sat behind the wheel – the car obeyed, backed away from the wall and came free. Then Karl swung it around and was ready to go.

The Butterfly was already on the way out.

'You've got it going already! We've got to get going. Where's Karl? Oh, sure, he's driving – '

Sissel also came out and stood beside him. He turned to her.

'Have you been in there?'

'Yes,' answered Sissel.

'I can see that you're of the same opinion as the others, but I can't help that – don't you understand that I've got to keep hoping as long as I can? Are you coming with us?

'No. Why?'

'No. Of course not. This is none of your affair. I just try to drag everybody around into it, that's just what I always do.'

'Somebody has to stay here,' said Sissel.

'Yes, I know. But you'll come with us?' he said to Olaf. 'You've got to come.'

'Yes,' replied Olaf.

'And Gudrun can come along. Where's Gudrun? Gudrun!' he shouted into the house.

Gudrun came out, she was pale and quiet. Olaf had never seen anything so beautiful as she was when she was pale and quiet. He caught her eye and was allowed to.

'Well, aren't we going to leave?' shouted Karl impatiently.

He had to shout in order to be heard over the noise of the motor. It appeared that he did not dare turn the engine off once it was going.

'Can we borrow some blankets?' he asked Sissel. It was Karl who had to make all arrangements, his father just fluttered around and chattered.

Sissel ran in after the blankets. Olaf caught a glimpse of the mid-wife who was helping get Kristine ready. He watched for a chance to be alone with her, then asked her if she had gone into Kristine's room any time during the night.

'No.'

'Not even when the house shook?'

'No, I wasn't ever in there before she was dead. But that crash was enough to scare the life out of anybody. Why?'

'Nothing.'

Olaf slipped away.

Dead, she had said, just like that.

Yes, the burden had fallen on Hjalmar and no one tried any longer to prevent him from making this trip, since he wished it.

He created a tense moment for them all while they were wrapping Kristine in the blankets in order to carry her out. They were all collected in her room except for Grete. He cleared his throat noisily to draw their attention to himself and then he stepped nervously before them. It was easy for them to see how much it was costing him, as he stood writhing before them.

'I can't keep quiet any longer,' he said.

They waited.

'What do you really think about all this?'

They had expected that. No one could answer.

'You've got to tell me!' he cried and they saw the perspiration glistening on his brow.

'We can't think anything about it!' spoke up Karl, in a hard tone of voice. They all understood why he used it.

'We've got to get finished with this now,' he added and turned away from his father.

The man continued:

'Do you think I've just gotten what I deserve, Karl?'

'We don't have time to talk about that now.'

Thank goodness Karl cut him off. They all stood there embarrassed.

'Do you think I'm standing here for my own amusement?' said the man. 'You know very well that I could have asked you that when we were alone, but I had to ask it in front of all the others.'

'Take a hold there,' Karl said nervously to Olaf.

Olaf fumbled and got hold. In back of him the voice kept up without pause:

'You won't answer. No one will answer. I'll never know – '

Karl finally flared up:

'It's been harder on some of the rest of us.'

'Who?'

Karl pointed at Kristine.

That was harsh. Karl regretted it immediately. The man started and looked imploringly at Olaf. Then at Sissel and Gudrun.

'Well, ready?' asked Karl, and they lifted Kristine up and carried her out between them. Her husband fluttered around and did not help. Sissel and Olaf helped carry. Outside the car was shaking and thundering.

'Will it go?' burst out of Sissel when she saw the damaged automobile.

'We've got to hurry,' buzzed the man.

'That's just what we've been doing,' answered Karl. 'We haven't used any more time than we had to.'

Karl was right. Actually they had used very little time. Hurrying back and forth. Working nervously while the man chattered away. Sissel came with more blankets so that they could pack them around and prop up the dead woman.

They placed her in the corner of the back seat. She sat there shaking, as if infused with life from the worn-out, noisy motor.

'Get in back,' Karl said curtly to his father.

The man obeyed.

Before Karl gave any more commands he ran into the house and called through the door to Grete:

'We're going now, Grete. We'll be back soon.'

They heard through the open doors the voice of the house's happy woman calling something back.

The man in the back seat said to Sissel who was standing beside the car:

'Will it soon be morning?'

'Yes.'

'But it doesn't feel like it.'

Sissel stared in amazement at him. The new morning was already breaking.

'Don't you hear the birds?'

'Birds?' he asked, confused.

They all listened a bit confused after Sissel's words: from the surrounding forest came the song of birds – the more they listened, the larger the chorus grew. They sang in the warm, cloudy morning.

Hjalmar shook his head as if he could not understand that he was listening to birds. The motor shook Kristine beside him. It was all he could do to hold the two things apart.

'Gudrun, come here,' he pleaded.

Gudrun was listening to the birds, together with Olaf. She went to him immediately.

'Sit down there.'

He pointed to the folding seat in front of him. The old car was roomy.

'You should really be sleeping,' he said when she had sat down.

'Pooh.'

He probably really only said it for the sake of appearances. This was the night when no one would sleep in that house.

Karl was ready now.

'Well, you might as well come along this time, too,' he said to Olaf, anxious to hold him. 'You've got to show us the way,' he used as a pretext.

That was good enough for Olaf. He scrambled into the front seat with Karl.

The older man in the back seat said:

'Olaf knows he has to come with us.'

Karl asked:

'But Gudrun? Is there any reason to take her along?'

'Gudrun has to come with us,' answered the man, frightened. 'What do we know about it – maybe she'll be just the one I need when we get there. No one knows. Don't you understand that I'll need every bit of support I can get?'

'Yes, yes.'

'Let's go then.'

He now made no claim to the wheel; his bubbling arrogance was gone.

Sissel stood back by the house. In Olaf's sleep-filled eyes she took the form of a strange, swaying flower in the familiar yard. It had been a turbulent night for her, now she stood there and was changed.

The car leaped forward with a roar.

28

LIKE A FLOWER she had stood there, he thought. A spell had been cast over his eyes. Gudrun sitting in the back of the car created a gentle enchantment.

Soon Tore will come, he thought.

Sissel was changed as she had stood there, fascinating and incomprehensible for him. A thought struck him: what would she do now?

It was all so tempting. Despite Kristine.

It was right to be taking a little trip out into the world, with Gudrun within arm's reach. He pushed aside all threatening thoughts connected with Kristine and the silence surrounding her and gave himself over to an illicit joy. Just a little, before Hjalmar started in with his impossible demands. Kristine was only like a door which has been slammed shut. He knew no more. I wish I could stop thinking about her, he thought – there are so many other things here for me.

'It's going beautifully,' said Karl and meant the battered, old car he was driving. Nothing had been damaged by the drastic measures required to get it going again. The old wreck chugged along obediently under Karl's hands.

'Yes, indeed,' his father answered. Then he sunk back down into the dark maze of problems he had to solve, or at least bear the night through.

Everything was silent as they drove along and passed houses. Only the birds showed signs of life. Everyone who had not received unexpected guests was still sleeping.

But soon a new day would break – and mother and father would come home. And as recently as yesterday afternoon Gudrun was nothing but a dream up in an attic window. Things could happen so quickly. But soon a new day would break –

'How is he? whispered Karl into his ear without taking his eyes off the road.

Olaf surreptitiously peeked into the back seat.

'He's just sitting there, holding her up.'

'Mmm. Thought so,' answered Karl.

'But keep an eye on him,' he mumbled to Olaf a little later.

Olaf did that gladly. Watched how the worn-out little man never grew tired. Now he was supporting the bundle with all his strength, took the shocks when the old flivver bounced, his brow was covered with perspiration and his cheeks were pale. Gudrun sat and stared at him and lifted him up out of his misery. She smiled at him and

Olaf was horrified to see that the man smiled back – as if he had been filled to overflowing. Where had that smile come from? Olaf learned a little about the efforts that must sometimes be made. If one is to hold out. Gudrun had already learned it and had had to use it. The man noticed Olaf and smiled at him. Olaf could not return the smile and turned around again – even though he had such a strange and good feeling inside him at the moment. They drove along like that.

Just what is it I'm supposed to do?

I guess I'll find out soon enough. Maybe it's nothing at all. He just talks nonsense all the time.

I've promised and promised, and that's all just nonsense, too. I don't have the slightest idea what I've promised.

But I want to be a part of this, he felt. I wouldn't have wanted this car to have driven past the house yesterday for anything in the world.

He looked back at Gudrun out of the corner of his eye.

Toss that lovely lock of hair, he wished.

No sooner had he thought it, than she did it. Then the lock fell forward over her brow again. Wasn't everything so changed and strange? She tossed the lock back in place again. But wasn't it all just like it should be!

Kristine lay in the corner and jiggled comfortably. There was no way to tell what the man was thinking, but he handled her the whole time as if she were still alive. Sissel had thoughtfully placed a towel over her face and no one had removed it.

They drove past houses and farms. Sleeping farms with sleeping fields. Wonderful fields that would have filled their lungs with a gentle sweetness if they had not been shut up inside a fume-filled automobile. Karl's car rattled through the countryside as if it possessed the will to reach their destination, to fulfill its mission. A few minutes earlier they had driven past the house where Olaf and

Karl had telephoned for the midwife, and now Olaf suddenly straightened up.

'Are we there soon?' asked Karl.

'Just around the next corner.'

29

ONCE INSIDE THE PREMATURELY awakened hospital they found out definitely that Kristine was dead. Her husband took the news without a word, without any reaction in particular. The drive to the hospital had prepared him after all. But they learned nothing definite about the cause of death. It was not easy to determine. She had not taken anything – but more could not be said. It was primarily her husband's own fault that the darkness surrounding her death was not probed into. It happened while the doctor was questioning them.

Olaf and Gudrun were sitting beside Hjalmar, giving him support. He began shaking violently. The doctor placed his questions carefully, but he did not receive any decent answers. Just shaking. Karl told in a few words all he knew about the night's events.

The doctor asked if they should send the dead woman to a hospital in the city for a complete autopsy, to a place fully equipped for such. In order to determine as exactly as possible the cause of her death.

'No!' said the man, and continued shaking.

The doctor gave up and left. Karl went quickly after him.

When the man was alone with Gudrun and Olaf he said to them in a frightened voice:

'I really do want to know. I just said that.'

Gudrun and Olaf tried to smile at him and be his servants, for he could not stand alone now. He half confided in them and asked:

'I don't *have* to know it, do I? But I want to.'

They knew nothing about it, but they both shook their heads. He said:

'It doesn't have to be because I crashed into the house!'

'No,' they said.

'No,' said Karl firmly. He had come back after his talk with the doctor.

'Did you hear that Karl said so, too?'

'He's in a bad way, you two'll have to take care of him,' Karl said out loud to them without caring if his father heard.

'What are you going to do?' asked Gudrun.

'Oh, I've got to make arrangements for both the living and the dead at the same time.'

Karl left.

'Don't you two go!' Hjalmar said.

They sat at his right and left hand and looked sympathetically at him. He was small and fluttery, and his usual ceaseless chattering had been interrupted for a while. Now he slowly began again.

'It's strange,' he said and began pulling and twisting at the arm of his jacket.

They waited.

'I was just thinking about how all this might have turned out different.'

He looked helplessly at Olaf.

'Yes,' answered Olaf obediently. He could feel the nearness of Gudrun and wished that they could remain sitting there a while longer.

'Just completely different. No one dead and nothing. Could just as well have turned out like that! It could just as well have just *barely* not turned out like it did. But why does it have to be this way?'

Neither of them answered.

'Isn't Karl coming back soon?'

'He's fixing things.'

'Yes, no one can fix things as well as Karl,' said the man and his face lit up.

'Did you see how I was shaking ?' he asked.

'Yes.'

'But now it's much better. And Karl fixed that with just a single word. Are you listening ?'

'Yes.'

'Yes indeed, what Karl says, does the most good after all. For you saw how I was shaking.'

30

THEY WERE SITTING in an ordinary empty and bare waiting room while Karl was out. A nurse on night-duty came in and said that everything necessary would be done with Kristine. She would be tended to and placed in a coffin, and it would be all right if she stayed there a couple of days if it would be best for them that way.

The man thanked the nurse. Olaf and Gudrun did not take their eyes off him, and he got through it well.

'So there's nothing more for us to do here ?'

'No.'

She started to leave.

'Oh, no, don't go,' he pleaded.

'Sorry, but I don't have time.'

'We're just waiting for Karl. Stay here until Karl comes back, if no longer. He'll be back in a minute.'

'Yes, but – '

'Can't you see what shape I'm in – '

'What's the matter ?' interrupted Gudrun.

Her father did not answer. But the way he looked made the nurse stay.

'Karl's getting the car ready,' Olaf informed them. 'I can see him from here.'

The man began arranging the chairs in the room in a straight row. Just could not sit still.

'I hope you'll excuse me,' he said to the nurse, 'and I'm sure you will.'

He looked at her with his friendly eyes.

A little later Karl came in. He was calm, and that helped. They could see that he had arranged everything, that. Grete was taken care of.

'Well, now we might as well drive home to Olaf's house,' he said, 'and get Grete. They'll send an ambulance for her a little later on in the morning.'

'I've got to stay here,' his father said.

'That's not necessary. They'll take care of Kristine here. There's no place for you to stay here, anyway.'

'I'm not budging.'

Karl looked confused and spoke softly to the nurse.

The nurse stepped forward and said that as far as they were concerned, it would be best if he left with the others.

'Well, all right,' he said, satisfied, 'as long as you say so.'

They noticed how a burden fell from his shoulders.

'I'm not afraid to stay here alone, don't go getting that idea,' he said. 'But I'm just as glad I don't have to.'

Now the nurse could leave.

The man stood still. They could see that something was brewing inside him. He must have been able to feel their friendliness toward him. He began speaking ceremoniously.

'Then we've gotten Kristine taken care of,' he began.

'Yes,' answered Karl. 'Now others will do the rest.'

'Well, she wasn't your mother, Karl, nor yours, either, Gudrun. She wasn't anybody's mother. But just the same – '

Then he stopped. But just the same, he had said. What more had he meant to say?

'There are things I regret, and they're eating at me something awful,' he began again, but was quickly interrupted by Karl:

'We don't want to hear anything about that.'

Karl said it curtly and firmly. Olaf was glad for that. He thought Gudrun was, too.

'Are you sure of that?' asked the man.

Karl said:

'Yes, we'd just as soon not hear about it. We've heard enough before, both Gudrun and I. We remember well enough what you two could say to each other. And you know just as well as I do that she wasn't really dumb yesterday. But we don't want to hear any more about it.'

At first the man did not answer. Olaf looked down at the floor and felt that he shouldn't have been there. Would Karl mention that she also could walk? He stood tensely waiting for it, but Karl said no more. Gudrun stood by her father's side and stared straight in front of her, but she stood as a defender on guard.

'I don't have to talk about it?' the man finally said.

'Are you glad for that?'

The man answered by beginning to shake again. Gudrun took his hand. But there was something he had to get out right away.

'Can you hear me?' he asked, as if they were surrounded by confusion and noise – although in reality there was not a sound.

'We're listening,' answered Karl.

'I just want to say: there are many things about what has happened that are not to be talked about from now on, that will just be left in peace. Is that what you mean, Karl?'

'That's right,' said Karl. 'And now quit worrying about it and stop shaking.'

The man's two young supporters were not old enough to take part in that, but they were witnesses to it and stood faithful and shining at his side.

The man continued:

'He who bears the guilt for it is happy and thankful that it can be done like that, so that I can walk among other people.'

'We'll not talk so much about that guilt. It was on both sides.'

The man fluttered and said one more thing:

'He who is left and still lives didn't choose that role. But he's glad for it.'

Karl straightened up and something hard came over him.

'What? Be quiet!'

His father jumped at the sight of him and the tone in his voice.

'All right, all right,' he mumbled and turned away.

'Excuse me,' Karl said.

Hjalmar let his breath out.

They went out of the waiting room. As they left they said good-bye to those members of the hospital's staff they happened to meet. But they would soon be back with Grete. Then they were outside in the new morning.

Once outside the man spoke to Karl with authority in his voice:

'From now on it's going to be different for you. Haven't you realized that?'

Karl nodded.

31

THEY ALL GATHERED around the car. Karl got it going again.

His father now lost that authority which had come over him at the moment Karl was struggling with his own weakness. Now he was listless and submissive.

He should have climbed into the car, but just stood and could not bring himself to it.

'It sure is funny. All I do is run away, no matter what I do.'

'Yes, but now we're going.'

'You could just as well listen to me a bit.'

'Not now,' Karl answered. 'Now we're going home to Olaf's house.'

The man climbed into the car. There was room in front beside Karl now. Olaf was sitting beside Gudrun in the back.

F

The man looked back at the hospital before they drove away.

'It sure is funny,' he repeated. 'If Kristine were here now, I think I'd have carried her a long way.'

The others wanted to look at each other, but instead sat as if they had not heard it.

'It's going!' the man shouted to Karl beside him and moved around restlessly although he was sitting in the car.

'All right, just calm down now. It's hard to drive when someone's always moving around.'

The father quieted down a bit. Karl drove as fast as the car would go.

In the back seat Gudrun and Olaf sat in the corners. The seat was wide and they were thin.

After a little while they were sitting close beside one another: Olaf had moved over.

He also happened to hold her hand. It was a strange and good feeling, so overtired and overstrained as he was.

'What are you doing that for now?'

He was startled by her casual tone of voice. It stood in such sharp contrast to what he himself was feeling. But soon the gentle mist settled around him once more and reshaped his vision and thoughts.

The sight of Hjalmar in the front seat was disturbing.

Gudrun whispered:

'What are you looking at Dad like that for?'

'Nothing,' he answered, content to hold her soft hand and just drive along.

Karl up front seemed to be calm and dependable now. But Olaf knew that he was not, it just appeared that way in comparison with his father's restless neck beside him.

A thought:

He's having a hard time of it.

And Gudrun is here –

Fumes from the motor poured in somewhere. But it made no difference. Unexpected and surprising things happened, too. Karl was struggling with something that had occurred to him, something his father had said earlier in the night – so that now his hard face softened: he said to his weary father, barely taking his eyes off the road:

'We're driving toward a little star, aren't we?'

Said it to his father who was hanging over a yawning abyss, but nonetheless had been the one who had formed the picture in his mind.

Then Karl's eyes were back on the road.

His father jumped as he sat there because Karl had said it so suddenly, looked around puzzled and said:

'Yes, and not just you.'

They could hear the defiance in his voice. *His* star was certainly not shining very brightly now.

Karl did not answer. His father was excited and had to continue:

'We all have one! Always and all the time. No matter how things look, we still do!'

They had no reply to that, but liked to hear him say it, each of them brought out small hidden stars they had and were driving toward.

Olaf felt Gudrun's lips against his ear:

'Did you hear that?'

What if this all disappears now? struck him suddenly right through the spell Gudrun cast.

Tonight, today anything can happen. When we get home, maybe the yellow house won't be there. We come to where it used to be, but there's only a large graceful angelica standing there bristling in the wind. A soft breeze is blowing, because the house had stood just there.

Sissel peeks out from behind the angelica. Is so small that she can hide behind a flower now.

No one can come here, she says.

But what about mother and father and the house?

And Karl steps forward:

Yes, and all I had here? Grete, and a little star that was mine?

They receive no answer.

Olaf stands with Gudrun beside the huge angelica and tells her all he knows about angelica –

'What are you thinking about?' he heard in his ear. 'Are you asleep?'

He woke up a little.

32

IT DID NOT TAKE THEM long to drive home in the early-morning hour, but still the features of the weary older man seemed to change during the trip. They must not say anything to him, thought Olaf.

They said nothing. Olaf sat holding Gudrun's hand and thought: do something. But what? What are you compared to him?

When they came to the bottom of the hill the house stood on, he could see the house standing there. More solid than in any dream.

'Stop here!' said the fluttery man.

He had become restless again. He put up his hand although he was sitting in a car.

'Stop!'

Karl jammed on the brakes.

'Is something wrong?'

'Yes.'

'Are you sick?'

'I want to get out here.'

He was a man who had come back pale from a drive.

Karl started to drive on.

'You can just as well drive up the hill with us.'

'Let me out here, Karl!'

The expression on his face stopped any further opposition, Karl opened the door and his father climbed out. He had grown thinner during the night. He grew thinner as they looked at him.

'I'm going for a walk alone,' he informed them. 'I've got something to think about.'

'All right,' said Karl.

The two in the back seat said nothing. Fatigue had begun humming through them again.

'I'll come up to the house soon,' promised the man. 'There's nothing to worry about. Don't worry about me. Just drive on.'

As if he did not belong with them. –

'You two go with him,' Karl said softly. 'He's in no shape to go wandering around alone.'

His ears appeared to be in good shape, however – he quickly caught the words.

'No, I've got to be alone. I promise to come up in a little while.'

They let him go and drove on up the hill. The racket they made would probably wake up anyone who might have fallen asleep at that weary morning hour. Perhaps they had not gone to sleep at all: Sissel came out immediately and was fresh and spruced up. She had changed clothes, too. She walked toward them and said nothing, but had changed her dress. A tiny morning wind breathed at her dress and played with it. Under it was all of Sissel's youth.

Although they had driven out of the yard with a dead woman, although a grim, silent drama had unfolded itself behind the closed door of her own room – Sissel still met them like that on their return. There was something indomitable in her.

Olaf watched Karl; he saw how the sight of Sissel swept across his face like a tired shadow. Something had slipped out of her grasp.

She noticed it in a glance, but she took it well, straightened up and walked erectly toward them. All of this happened before a word was spoken.

Sissel had to ask:

'How did it go?'

'She was dead,' answered Olaf in a voice the others could barely hear.

'How's everything here?' asked Karl, almost like a command. He did not wait for an answer, but walked past her and into the house.

Gudrun followed him. Just outright followed Karl her brother, her head lifted. Olaf wanted to try somehow to stop her, but Gudrun did not stop, just walked away without explanation. She was changed when she was near Sissel.

Olaf and Sissel were left standing beside the car. Olaf stepped close to her, tried to recapture something of what had been there before. It was no longer there. Sissel cleared her throat and asked about the trip.

'And now they'll all have to leave in a little while,' Olaf said in closing.

'Well, that's their privilege.'

They stood there and knew many things about each other.

'When it really gets to be daytime an ambulance will come and take Grete to the hospital.'

Olaf felt the words smarting. Deep in his own thoughts, he said after a while:

'Why does it have to be that way?'

Gave no further explanation.

'With what?'

'Nothing.'

He just felt that he would never again meet that Gudrun-up-in-the-window. She no longer existed.

33

THEN THE HOUSE BEGAN to rock with fatigue. The tension was now temporarily released – and the accompanying prickling joy had also seeped away, in vain. Then came a sudden dip down into sleep. It was really about the time one usually wakes up.

Olaf and Sissel had once again sat down on the sofa in the living room, and then the room began to tilt. Sissel sat stiffly as if she were trying to keep from sliding down a steep bank. Sleep hummed and tempted inside Olaf. No sound was to be heard from the room where Karl and Grete were.

The house tilted more, but in a good and secure way. Olaf stretched out and lay his head in Sissel's lap. She twined her fingers in his hair. Olaf was startled by a thought:

We've just been dreaming it all!

He looked around, dazed by sleep. There was not a trace of any strangers to be seen. Only he and his sister were there, just as it was supposed to have been that night.

Well, you're here, anyway, he thought.

'Sissel – '

'– is it ?' she said sleepily.

'Have we just been dreaming this ?'

'About these people ?'

'Yes, that they've been here ?'

She shook her head.

'You're so tired that you can't think straight any longer, Olaf. They're not far away.'

He dozed off again. Of course they were here. This sleepiness had come at the moment Gudrun walked away without a word of explanation.

Through a patch of mist he heard Sissel's voice:

'You came back to me, anyway.'

'Yes. Have you been dreaming, too ?'

'We haven't been dreaming.'

There was bitterness in her voice. He couldn't figure it out. Sleep was humming too loudly.

34

THE CAR HORN began blaring just outside the house.

Olaf was pulled abruptly back from sleep. The sound seemed to cut to the marrow.

He still lay with his head in Sissel's lap. She had probably been dozing herself while he had been sleeping.

'What was that?'

'It's that man, he's fluttered around and gotten hold of the car horn.'

Of course. Now he recognized the sound.

'I saw him come up the hill and begin fooling around with the car,' Sissel said.

'Haven't you been sleeping?'

'I don't know.'

She brushed the question away, busy watching the restless man outside the window.

'I guess he's not finished with us yet, from the sound of it,' she said.

Then it all came back. There stood the car with its smashed front. The horn was blaring. The man who had carried so faithfully was flitting around as before. Now he was desperately blowing the horn, sending out a warning signal. His head was never at rest out there. They seemed to hear his chattering and buzzing.

The tension and excitement flamed up in Olaf's consciousness, renewed. And in his muscles – his body was awake. His dip into sleep had ended with renewal for the second time that night. He once more was ready to participate in whatever might happen.

Something similar must have happened to Sissel. She sat up straight and a firmness came over her body. The horn outside was calling and the man somehow made it sound so that they understood that it was coming from another and more difficult existence than theirs.

'What the devil is he doing to make it sound like that?'

'Well, just so long as he doesn't get it going and crash into the house again,' said Sissel.

'That's just what he's trying to do – '

'Listen!'

The horn sounded again. Was it because they could not properly judge sounds after the sleepless night, or did the man actually have the power to make it sound so blaringly loud and insistent.?

What was he calling for?

Olaf thought: Do I have to go out and tell about the shade that was drawn down? No, I can't. He's decreed that what has happened is never more to be mentioned, Olaf said firmly to himself.

But peace did not come.

Listen –

That horn calling forth old anxieties – what did it mean?

'What do you think it means, Sissel?'

Olaf stammered a little, gripped by it. Sissel answered only:

'He can't be all there.'

But the words were harmless. They knew very well that he was as sane as anyone else.

'Now they've heard it, too.'

They heard excited voices in the bedroom.

The horn had sounded through all the rooms. The door to the bedroom was opened with a jerk, and Karl came out. He was real enough, Olaf had not just dreamed him. He must have been sleeping a little, too; he had taken his jacket off. Behind him could be glimpsed the wonderful picture of Grete and her baby. Others could be seen: the midwife, Gudrun. Grete had the baby. Karl was coming from that now.

He called over his shoulder:
'You don't have to come, Gudrun.'
It was a sharp order.
The door slammed shut.

Gudrun shouldn't even come out? Karl took the honking he had heard that seriously.

Karl asked as he ran through the room, without looking at them:
'What's he doing, anyway?'

'He's honking the horn.'

'We were sleeping, and the first thing we knew the horn was blowing,' said Olaf.

Before Karl got outside the signal sounded once more. Flowed through those he was calling. Karl turned to Olaf and Sissel: 'Come on,' he said. 'You might as well come, too.'

Karl spoke softly, but they followed him immediately. Karl was now outside. He walked over to the car and opened the door. Sissel and Olaf could see that he was very calm. They had now also reached the yard.

Hjalmar sat in the driver's seat. Had sent out a few alarming signals.

'Have you come back now?' asked Karl calmly. 'You were gone quite a while. We've been relaxing a bit up here.'

Sissel grasped Olaf's arm the moment she saw the older man up close.

No wonder the horn had sounded as it did.

Karl spoke casually:
'Did you want something?'

The man looked as if he could hardly understand such a question.
'I was just calling,' he answered.

His restlessness was not noticeable now. When he was under the greatest stress it disappeared. This was also the reason Karl could talk to him without becoming infuriated.

They waited for an explanation. The man looked like he did not think it was necessary to give one. Karl let it pass unnoticed, said calmly:

'Come out of the car now, Dad. You'll just wake everyone up too early with that honking.'

'Not everybody wakes up so easily this morning,' replied the man.

'No, that's true.'

'Yes, it sure is,' said the man. 'And isn't that a good enough reason? For me?'

'Of course it is,' answered Karl.

Sissel and Olaf glanced at each other and wished they were far away. Just so long as he didn't start blowing that crazy horn again.

Karl undoubtedly had the same wish:

'Come on out of the car now, Dad. There's a bed ready for you inside. It may be quite a while before the ambulance comes for Grete.'

'I'm not tired.'

'And just what were you honking the horn for?'

The man could give no adequate explanation.

'I was just sitting out here by myself.'

'Well, don't go blowing that horn and scaring yourself anymore,' Karl said. 'Come on out now or I'll drag you out!'

He carried out his threat, reached into the car and took hold of the weak man. It took next to nothing to pull him away from the steering wheel and the horn. He came out of the car and was so exhausted that he sat right down on the ground.

'Where's Gudrun?'

'Inside.'

'Gudrun!' shouted the father.

Gudrun came out so quickly that she must have been standing waiting for the call.

Hjalmar brightened up.

'Just look at that! Look at Gudrun!'

The others looked at her in amazement. Saw nothing new about her. Her father must have been looking at her with different eyes.

'What's the matter, Dad?'

'I want you here.'

She asked for no further explanation. Was used to his ways. Olaf tried to recapture her. She responded and stopped close by him. He made a tiny motion in return and thought:

Everything's all right after all –

It was her father who had carried and carried for a whole year – now he was trying to collect himself. He succeeded in holding his hands still. When he had finally gotten control over his restless body, he raised his voice without chattering and began a kind of roll call – there in the yard which was not allowed to be in peace.

'Karl,' he called out and began with the largest and darkest.

'Yes?'

'Gudrun,' he continued. That name which he had given her himself. He said it in just that way, too.

'Yes,' she answered. 'Here I am.'

She said it warmly and softly and was standing right beside Olaf. He wished their eyes could meet and that with them they could lift up this miserable man as they had done when they first saw each other the evening before. But now Gudrun was turned blindly toward her father, waiting to fulfill his wishes.

'And then you two, who've gotten mixed up in my affairs,' he said, turning toward Sissel and Olaf.

'Yes?' they answered unconsciously, mechanically, because it was a roll call.

The man gathered them all together with his eyes and said:

'I blew the horn, as you heard, and I'm sure you know what I meant by it. Yes, I can see that you know, right through everything you say and ask about and hide it with.'

They grew uncomfortable. The tone he used turned it into an accusation against them. Karl spoke up:

'Yes, you see what you want to see, just like everyone else. But you can't shove any of this off on us.'

The man looked frightened at Karl.

'I've never thought of shoving anything off on anybody.'

Karl could not accept that.

'Are you trying to drag us all into what's happened?' he said in a hard voice.

'No.'

'That's the way it sounds to me, and I won't have any of it.'

His exhausted father answered:

'I'm just trying to fight for my life.'

As he said that, a faint coloring spread through his face. It disappeared again immediately.

'Maybe *you* have to, too, Karl,' he continued. 'I blew the horn to remind you of that.'

Karl laughed bitterly:

'You don't have to remind me of anything.'

'But you've already changed so much,' his father said. 'I'm the one who won't find anyone when I go in.'

It chilled them to listen to him. Karl stepped over to Olaf and said in a low voice:

'Take your sister and get away from this. Go to bed and try to get a little sleep – or just go, at any rate. He has no right to pull others into it. Gudrun and I are used to this sort of thing. But you two should be spared it.'

The man understood immediately what Karl was doing even without hearing what he said.

'It's no use, Karl. They've got to be here and help pass judgement.'

Olaf and Sissel were a bit startled.

Hjalmar turned to them:

'Are you going to leave? I've got to find out what you know about Kristine.'

'I don't know anything,' said Sissel.

Olaf kept silent. He had not been asked so directly that he had to answer. Something was delicately balanced. Something in the brother and sister would have welcomed a chance to get away. But Gudrun interfered, moved in on them:

'Please don't leave him when he's like this. He can take so little. Please stay here with him – '

They could hear that she was frightened. She had the power to sort of bend them together – Sissel and Olaf and herself, so that they became a unity, a tranquil fortress.

'Please don't leave me, either,' she said.

Olaf and Sissel were struck by how lonely Gudrun was. Sissel said softly and unsteadily:

'We're not going to go.'

'No,' said Olaf breathlessly. 'We won't go.'

Olaf now realized that Gudrun had not walked away without explanation. Now she was back again.

The man started in again:

'Time and time again today I've called people together – '

It stopped. He was not able to continue.

'Well, what do you want with us now,' asked Karl impatiently.

'Don't you understand? But it's not your affair now, that's so.'

'Don't you remember what you said we were driving toward today?' he continued.

'Of course,' Karl answered, puzzled.

'Don't you think I could use some sort of little star, too?' the man said almost in desperation.

Karl did not answer.

'I can't leave this and go toward nothing. You should be able to understand that, Karl.'

'Well, then I'll remind you about what you said: you said that everybody has one as long as they live.'

'Well – ' said the man.

'So I just don't believe you when you say that you're going toward nothing. Why do you have to carry on like this and just make things hard for yourself, anyway?' Karl ended irritably.

The man turned away. He caught sight of Sissel and turned toward her:

'As you can see, a person's not asked about what he's going to get mixed up in.'

'No, that's true,' answered Sissel. 'Olaf and I weren't given any warning about this night.'

'Yes, everybody thinks about himself,' the man said.

'Excuse me,' said Sissel, ashamed.

'No need to. But what do you think about what happened to Kristine in that closed room?'

Sissel unconsciously reached out for her brother at this sudden question. Shook her head. The man continued:

'No. Well, you're probably not close enough to it. But why did it have to happen tonight? Today was the day I was going to make up with her.'

Sissel looked around in confusion at the others. Her eyes rested on Karl who made her shy and ashamed of herself, but who she still in a way was constantly turned toward and on guard against.

Karl saw her look and quickly interfered.

'Are you still at it?' he said to his father. 'We don't know anything about that! You'll never find out about it if you don't have the answers yourself. Are you so sure that you would have done it today? And wasn't it you who decided that all this was never to be discussed any more?'

His father answered:

'That was a wish. What you wish for often becomes suddenly something quite different, it feels different before you even know it. I blew the horn because I'm fighting for my life, I said.'

'Yes, yes, you've told us that. You've told us too much.'

The man began flapping.

'Too much? This is nothing for you, Karl, you who've made it through, right here in this same house. I can see in your eyes that you don't have anything to say as far as any need is concerned. And that's a good thing, too, but just the same – '

Karl did not reply.

The man returned to Sissel:

'If there's one thing that's sure, it's that Kristine was dead right when I was thinking of going in to her and making up. I was on the way. Isn't that strange?'

Sissel was disturbed and answered reluctantly:

'We don't know anything about it all.'

'Child,' said the man. 'No one chooses what comes tumbling down on his head.'

155

Olaf saw how Sissel was both irritated and ashamed. It was like the man had said, you were not asked beforehand. But what about them who pushed it onto you? Olaf thought resentfully. Was that beside the point, too? Child, he had said, that flutterer who had brought it all down on them.

'Anyway, I was never in there!' said Sissel. 'So you can just leave me alone.'

Olaf stared shocked at Sissel. She must have been worn out, and besides, Karl was standing so close to her – she had worked herself up to using a screeching tone of voice that was unlike her and made her seem pathetic. Shabby and pathetic. Olaf looked at her while the dread of the coming questioning tortured him. It would soon be his turn. The man stood there tormenting Sissel; it was only a short postponement. He was perspiring and frightened, his stomach felt cramped.

The man paid no attention to the negative answer he had received from Sissel, but pressed her even harder. She was tired and frightened and resorted to unthought-of things in self-defense.

'Ask Olaf!' she cried out. 'He was in there.'

'No!' she added in the same breath.

Olaf threw everything up. At the moment Sissel said that, his stomach turned and he saw spots before his eyes. He barely managed to dash wildly around to the other side of the car. There he could loosen the knot. He clutched the car door.

Sissel was after him immediately.

'Are you sick?'

She diverted her eyes as she spoke.

'No, it was just – now I've gotten rid of it.'

'I didn't mean to say that, Olaf! I didn't mean it. But I'm so tired I didn't know what I was saying. You hear?'

'Yes.'

'Do you believe me?'

'Yes.'

'What's the matter?' called Karl across the battered car.

'Nothing,' answered Sissel. 'It's all right now.'

'Here,' she said and handed Olaf something to dry his mouth with. Then they went back. Olaf felt like a baby. There stood Karl, and there was his father in the same belligerent position as before.

Karl took his father by the arm.

'You just hold up now. She's right, they don't have to answer anything about why Kristine died last night.'

The man pulled himself free.

'I think I have a perfect right to ask whoever I want. Everyone has something to answer.'

Olaf felt terrible. He did not dare turn toward this man who was not to be evaded. In the midst of his fear he was irritated over seeing Sissel standing there looking so shabby. Shabby was the last thing Sissel should be. The morning light was sharp and showed her in all her poverty. She shouldn't look like that. For she wasn't like that, it was a lie.

The man paid no attention to any opposition when it came to getting information about Kristine; there he came. Olaf saw him coming and tried desperately to find something to say. He was on the point of vomiting again.

'Is it true what your sister says, that you know more about Kristine than we do?'

'I don't know,' answered Olaf.

What'll I do? he thought. He felt many eyes fastened on him, tried to find Sissel's among them, but did not like them when he had found them, they were so repenting and shameful.

The man fluttered a bit when he began again.

'You should pay attention when a man in my shape asks you something. You're big enough to understand it all, you can't hide behind anything. You were the last person to see Kristine alive and that's why everything you can tell me is important. And she talked to you, too – because she wasn't made dumb in the car yesterday.'

157

He stopped and looked compellingly at Olaf.

Olaf felt a heavy burden of things he knew. And one thing before all others: that she had gotten out of bed and drawn the shade, she who had been carried for a whole year.

'Yes,' he said.

'Yes what?'

'That she could talk.'

'That's no secret, but what did she say?'

Olaf jumped at the one thing that was nice to be able to tell:

'She said that she was waiting – '

'For me to come?' interrupted the man.

'Yes.'

'Did you hear that?' the man said deliriously. 'She was waiting for me!'

He was once more above being irritating and wearying. The information seemed to stir up a wild tumult inside him. He took a turn around the car. Beside himself.

Karl whispered hurriedly to Olaf:

'Not a word about that she could walk – if she mentioned it. He's known it all along – and never said a word about it. He can't stand any talk about it.'

'But – '

'He couldn't take hearing it mentioned. That's why he's carried for a whole year.'

Olaf shivered, both from Karl's words and the feeling of relief that the secret of the shade should remain a secret.

The man tried to collect himself, and said to Olaf:

'Well, I won't bother you any more. Now that I've found that out – but just think of it: just when I was on my way to her! And now she's not there.'

Perhaps without realizing it he was still threatening Olaf and Sissel. In boundless poverty. Karl had to interfere.

'You said you wouldn't bother them anymore – and now you're at it again. They don't have anything to do with it.'

'How. can you stand there and say that, Karl?' asked his father. 'Where would you have been if we had treated you like that: not listened to you when you came home wounded? We never once said that we didn't have anything to do with it.'

'That was different, you're my father. And now I think you can just stop it.'

'You don't know anything about it!'

Karl said, with authority in his voice:

'I know quite a bit about it. So now I'm just going to tell you something! You don't have to be afraid that you haven't made it up, Dad. You've carried and carried and made it up so that I'll never be able to forget it. I think you can have that to your credit.'

They all looked at Karl. They gladly looked at him. His father was the first to look at him. It grew quiet. They felt that a vital and soothing judgement had been passed.

35

IT'S A FINE MORNING, they suddenly thought.

'I want to do something,' mumbled the man and began with his fluttering and chattering again. 'You can just go ahead and think what you want, but I want to blow the horn. So please let me into the car.'

The last words were said to Sissel who was standing beside the car door. Sissel moved away with a little bow she had never thought of making. Just made it.

'Come on now, no more honking,' said Karl and interfered. 'Come out of there.'

The man obediently came out. Then he looked at Olaf.

'You told me a wonderful thing after all, Olaf. I want to thank you for that. And what happened last of all, what nobody saw, I'll find that out, too.'

Karl was keeping a suspicious eye on him. But Olaf was just happy.

'There's a long road ahead,' chattered the man. 'I thought we could get it all settled right here. But I'll find out about what's left if I have to wade through fire and water. I won't rest until it's all cleared up!'

He was showing off and talking big, but he still did not seem ridiculous. Karl did not interfere and say that he was just making it hard for himself. They knew that he would never be able to find out what had happened in that closed room, but he for some reason did not become ridiculous because he insisted that he would. When they thought about what he had had the strength to do during the past year they believed in him. Although he could hardly stand on his feet after that night, and his hands were never at rest.

Instead of Hjalmar's insistent honking, they heard a short, businesslike honk down on the road. A large ambulance swung into the driveway.

The fluttering man stopped short, with arms hanging loosely at his sides, at the height of his burst of rapture.

'What's that?'

'The ambulance coming for Grete and the baby,' Karl answered calmly. 'I arranged for it. They said they'd come as soon as it was morning.'

'Oh, sure. I'd forgotten all about it,' said the man.

'So now it's morning for everyone!' he continued. 'Now we'll be leaving.'

Olaf felt the words clutch at his heart. But nothing could be stopped. The light-grey ambulance climbed the hill with calm strength, and could not be stopped by a hidden wish. Would all of this disappear now? Yes, what else? Gudrun was already running into the house to tell Grete and the midwife.

The ambulance stopped alongside Karl's stubborn old wreck. Two husky men pulled out a stretcher. They laughed and talked with Karl. Hjalmar flitted around and looked on helplessly. They looked him over quickly, but grinned more at the car.

'Maybe you don't think it'll go?' asked Hjalmar.

'Right in here,' Karl said quickly.

They hurried into the house, at Karl's heels. The older man fluttered along after them, mumbling something about people he had to talk with. It looked like he did not especially care to be left alone with Olaf and Sissel now.

Suddenly they were standing alone.

It's strange.

Why is it like this?

They looked quickly at each other. Something was weighing on Sissel, she stepped closer:

'Olaf – '

He knew very well what it was.

'Yes?' he answered reluctantly.

'I didn't mean to do what I did before, really! You know I never go telling on you like that. It just popped out before I knew it.'

'Ahh – ' he shrugged, embarrassed.

That was over. They stood together silently. Felt a nameless smarting.

36

'SURE IS BUSY AROUND HERE,' said a familiar voice right in back of them before they had a chance to catch their breath.

Tore.

'Where did you come from?' asked Sissel hostilely.

'Good morning,' was all he replied, as if the coming of the morning were enough to explain his presence.

Tore's clothes were quite bedraggled after the night of rain and wet forest groves, but there was nothing bedraggled in his eyes – even if they were full of sleep, they rested intently on Sissel.

'I've been here,' he said in answer to her question.

'Here?'

He waved his arms in a wide circle. For the sake of appearances only, because she knew all about it since he had met Olaf earlier in the night.

'Right around here,' he said.

Sissel looked away.

'Really?' she said in a bored voice.

'Yes, but I wanted to see the end of this. This circus here.'

'Oh?'

'Anyway I met Olaf a while back and told him to tell you I was coming.'

She continued looking away.

'I can see he told you.'

'Oh?'

'Well, it looks like they'll finally be leaving now,' continued Tore casually.

Sissel tossed her head sharply.

'What do you know about it, about any of it? You can just leave!'

He was not the same Tore he had been yesterday. He had changed, too.

'Sissel – ' he said and touched her arm. In a tone of voice that shot through Olaf. A tone he had never heard before. A tone that swelled up through him.

Then Tore turned and walked away. Erectly and lightly. Changed. But not defeated. Quite to the contrary.

Olaf did not dare look at Sissel. He hurried away. Into the house. Sissel followed him. He heard and saw it before him:

Sissel – Tore had said and touched her.

A shock had run swiftly through all of Sissel's being.

37

I KNOW ALL about you and Tore, he intended to say to Sissel as soon as he had a chance.

Shut up, Olaf! she would answer.

But he was sure she'd soon be Tore's. He did not feel the least bit of animosity toward him. In a little while he would be back. It *was* Tore now.

As he entered the living room he heard noises of confusion and excited talking in Grete's room. They were all in there getting Grete ready to move her out into the ambulance.

Sissel had not followed him after all. Through the window he could see her still standing outside in the morning air. As if she were filling up on blood and life after the recent shame of having betrayed him to the fluttering man to save herself. She'll soon be Tore's, he thought blindly.

Gudrun came toward him.

That was right and natural.

Right and natural, but still he felt a thick and dangerous thumping begin in his throat. He moved quickly into one corner of the room, so that Sissel outside could not see him. Gudrun could follow him, and she did. She was troubled and looked down at the floor. Troubled for the first time since she had come.

'I saw you come in – '

'Oh?'

'And so I knew you were alone.'

'Yes.'

'Well, we're going to leave now.'

Olaf nodded.

Why does it have to be like this? he could have asked, but not to Gudrun.

'I – I wish you could stay longer,' he stammered out.

Strange, indistinct thoughts raced back and forth in his brain. Should he remind her of something? That they measured arms in the middle of the night?

She was standing very close to him and he touched her, like Tore had touched Sissel outside – he could feel he was blushing. She was going to leave now, but she could come back, couldn't she? She can write to me.

She said nothing. Was not her usual self.

'It sure is funny,' he said and smiled, unsure of himself. 'Remember how we measured arms?'

'Yes.'

She did not say it as he had thought she would. Yes, was all she had said. In a flash he understood that he was on the wrong track. Was it just his own confused thinking?

'You could write to me!' he said impulsively, desperately.

'Write?'

It was difficult for her to make her voice sound.

'What'll I write about?'

Another shock.

'Couldn't you?'

'We'll see,' she answered.

'Isn't there anything?' he asked in despair. He could find no other words to express it – but though only thirteen years old, she understood it immediately.

'No – ' she said and blushed.

To be safe she put her hands behind her back.

'What?' he said softly, as his head whirled. But then he saw that she had her hands behind her back, and that was clear enough.

'But I sat right beside your bed, and – ' he said as if to insist on some sort of right. He felt hurt, too.

'Oh, sure, but that's nothing so special,' replied Gudrun.

What?

He had been blinded when she had first appeared the preceding evening and been Gudrun-up-in-the-window come to life. And the blindness had stayed with him. Everything she had said and done meant nothing.

She asked:

'Are you angry?'

'Angry? No!' he said and snorted.

If he only could have told her how it all was: about Gudrun from his world of make-believe who had been given flesh and blood.

'What are you going to do now, then?' he asked. That much he had a right to know.

She did not answer. Just stood there, turned away from him. But he had to find out and asked demandingly:

'What are you going to do now? From now on?'

'Keep an eye on the Butterfly,' she answered quickly and motioned toward the bedroom.

Olaf had not expected that, and had no answer ready.

Then what was troubling her came out:

'We're just a nuisance wherever we are.'

He did not answer. Later he regretted it. A nuisance? Never!

She had to go.

'So long,' she said, and kept her hands behind her back so that there would be no danger of any misunderstanding.

'So long,' he answered.

She was still blushing. He liked that.

She turned and went into the bedroom where they were noisily getting ready to leave – his last meeting with Gudrun had not lasted very long, but he could feel it. He watched her fine, quick legs disappear through the doorway and struggled with a far from grown-up sob somewhere inside him.

Sissel came in instead, filled with her troubles. But she still had her eyes open.

'What are you and Gudrun doing? You've been standing here together a long time. Are you sweethearts now?'

He gave it to her good:

'Oh, shut up!'

38

GRETE WAS READY NOW. Sissel had also gone in to help – and now they all came out. Through the living room and out into the hall and out into the yard without stopping.

When they first appeared, it resembled a funeral procession – but it rapidly changed into a caravan of life. Grete, lying on her stretcher, was responsible for that. She looked joyously and frankly around her. Karl came first, to hold the doors open.

Olaf had intended to stay inside, but he was pulled along.

The fluttery man was in front and in back and everywhere. Sissel and Gudrun came last, together with the midwife.

The man chattered away.

'Well, now we're leaving *this* house. Yes, indeed, lots of things sure are different from yesterday – and not just for me – '

'Yes, yes,' said Karl to try to cut him off.

The man looked around, as if taking in the morning in that place.

'Kristine passed away one spring night. Isn't that strange? That someone should pass away in the middle of a spring night?'

'Yes, yes, yes,' said Karl up front.

'Well, we're going now, Olaf!' said the man loudly, displeased at having been interrupted. 'And like I said, what you couldn't tell me, I'll find out myself. I won't rest until I do! I'll hardly eat or sleep – '

He appeared to be on top at the moment. Olaf had nothing to answer.

'Give me your hand,' Grete said to him as she was being carried out, and stretched her free arm out from under the blanket.

He obeyed gladly.

'Well, now you two can finally go to bed, too,' Grete said. 'Thanks a lot, Olaf.'

Gudrun nodded to him in passing. She had already said goodbye.

Sissel also was bidden farewell, but did not get through it so easily. But that would take care of itself. Grete was placed in the ambulance and disappeared completely.

'I want to drive with you, so I'll be sure to get there!' said Hjalmar and scrambled and fluttered up onto the driver's seat in the ambulance. 'I've had enough of old flivvers,' he added.

The old wreck of a car began thundering. Karl had climbed in and Gudrun was sitting beside him. He nodded to Olaf as the car started rolling down the hill:

'Maybe we'll meet again when you're grown up. Go to bed now and get some sleep.'

ALSO BY TARJEI VESAAS
PUBLISHED BY PETER OWEN

THE BIRDS

Translated from the Norwegian by Torbjørn Støverud and Michael Barnes
0 7206 1143 1 • Paperback • 224pp • £9.95

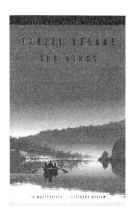

A tale of delicate beauty and simplicity by one of the greatest Scandinavian writers of the twentieth century, *The Birds* tells the story of the mentally unstable Mattis, who lives in a small house near a lake with his sister Hege, who ekes out a modest living knitting sweaters. From time to time she encourages her brother to find work to ease their financial burdens, but Mattis's attempts come to nothing. When, finally, he sets himself up as a ferryman, the only passenger he manages to bring across the lake is a lumberjack, Jørgen. But when Jørgen and Hege become lovers Mattis finds he cannot adjust to this new situation and complications abound.

'A masterpiece.' – *Literary Review*

'A spare, icily humane story . . . The character of Mattis, absurd and boastful but also sweet, pathetic and even funny, is shown with great insight.' – *Sunday Times*

'True visionary power.' – *Sunday Telegraph*

'A beautiful and subtle novel, which combines the bleakest pessimism with a broad and rich response to both human feeling and to landscape.' – *Scotsman*

'A story of delicate beauty.' – London *Evening Standard*

'*The Birds* is a delight.' – *European*

'Disarmingly insightful . . . masterful economy.' – *Tablet*

ALSO BY TARJEI VESAAS
PUBLISHED BY PETER OWEN

THE BOAT IN THE EVENING

Translated from the Norwegian by Elizabeth Rokkan
0 7206 1198 9 • Paperback • 184pp • £9.95

A series of semi-autobiographical sketches, *The Boat in the Evening* evokes intensely poetic scenes with cinematic beauty: a colony of cranes arrive at their mating ground to play out a delicate ritual drama; a boy and his father clear a road together in a pitiless snowstorm; a drowning man floats down river towards rescue.

Vesaas felt the book, which has drawn favourable comparisons with the work of T.S. Eliot and Wordsworth, to be the culmination of his life's experience. Indeed, this profound and beautiful novel, with its sensuous appreciation of nature, was to be his last published work.

'A clear crystal of imagination . . . a rare kind of masterpiece.' – *Daily Telegraph*

'The several lonelinesses that can exist within a family; the effect on the emotions of the living presences of trees, grass, water; the half-understood nature of the adult world to a child: all these Vesaas conjures brilliantly from the sombre north.' – *Times Literary Supplement*

'A rare mixture of creative vitality, conviction and artistry.' – *Guardian*

'An excellent translation by Elizabeth Rokkan catches the quiet, poetic mood.' – *Sunday Telegraph*

'Disturbing and beautiful . . . elaborate and powerful.' – *Sunday Times*

'A book of great strength and beauty.' – *The Times*

ALSO BY TARJEI VESAAS
PUBLISHED BY PETER OWEN

THE ICE PALACE
Translated from the Norwegian by Elizabeth Rokkan
0 7206 1122 9 • Paperback • 176pp • £9.95

Siss and Unn are new friends — so new that they have spent only one whole evening in each other's company. But so profound is that evening that when Unn inexplicably disappears, Siss's world is shattered. Siss's struggle with her fidelity to the memory of her friend and Unn's fatal exploration of the strange, terrifyingly beautiful frozen waterfall that is the ice palace are described in prose of a lyrical economy that ranks among the most memorable achievements of modern literature.

In 1973 Vesaas received the highly prestigious Nordic Council Prize for *The Ice Palace*.

'How simple this novel is. How subtle. How strong. How unlike any other. It is unique. It is unforgettable. It is extraordinary.' – Doris Lessing, *Independent*

'It is hard to do justice to *The Ice Palace* . . . The narrative is urgent, the descriptions relentlessly beautiful, the meaning as powerful as the ice piling up on the lake.' – *The Times*

'Vesaas's laconic sentences are as cold and as simple as ice – and as fantastic.' – *Daily Telegraph*

'Austere poetical clarity, stoical wisdom and a vivid response to nature.' – *Times Literary Supplement*

'Believable and haunting . . . the beautiful neo-prose poem is as sombre and Scandinavian as a Bergman film.' – *Nova*

If you have enjoyed this book you may like to read some of the other Peter Owen paperback reprints listed below. The Peter Owen Modern Classics series was launched in 1998 to bring some of our internationally acclaimed authors and their works, first published by Peter Owen in hardback, to a new readership.

To order books or a free catalogue or for further information on these or any other Peter Owen titles, please contact the Sales Department, Peter Owen, 73 Kenway Road, London SW5 0RE, UK tel: + 44 (0)20 7373 5628 or + 44 (0)20 7370 6093, fax: + 44 (0)20 7373 6760, e-mail: sales@peterowen.com or visit our website at www.peterowen.com.

Title	Author	ISBN (0 7206)	Price £
The Butcher's Wife	Li Ang	1161 X	9.95
Kappa	Ryunosuke Akutagawa	1200 4	9.95
Les Onze Mille Verges	Guillaume Apollinaire	1100 8	9.95
Midnight Mass	Paul Bowles	1083 4	9.95
Their Heads Are Green	Paul Bowles	1077 X	9.95
Points in Time	Paul Bowles	1137 7	7.99
Up Above the World	Paul Bowles	1087 7	9.95
Plain Pleasures	Jane Bowles	1178 4	9.95
Two Serious Ladies	Jane Bowles	1179 2	9.95
Confessions of Dan Yack	Blaise Cendrars	1158 X	8.95
Dan Yack	Blaise Cendrars	1157 1	9.95
Gold	Blaise Cendrars	1175 X	8.95
To the End of the World	Blaise Cendrars	1097 4	9.95
The Astonished Man	Blaise Cendrars	1210 1	9.95
My Life	Marc Chagall	1186 5	9.95
Le Livre Blanc	Jean Cocteau	1081 8	8.50
The Miscreant	Jean Cocteau	1173 3	9.95
Duo and Le Toutounier	Colette	1069 9	9.95
Pope Joan	Lawrence Durrell	1065 6	9.95
In the Shadow of Islam	Isabelle Eberhardt	1191 1	9.95
The Samurai	Shusaku Endo	1185 7	9.95
Wonderful Fool	Shusaku Endo	1080 X	9.95
Silence	Shusaku Endo	1211 X	10.95
Urien's Voyage	André Gide	1216 0	8.95
Two Riders on the Storm	Jean Giono	1159 8	9.95
To the Slaughterhouse	Jean Giono	1212 8	9.95

Title	Author	ISBN (0 7206)	Price £
Demian	Herman Hesse	1130 X	9.95
Gertrude	Herman Hesse	1169 5	9.95
Journey to the East	Herman Hesse	1131 8	7.99
Narcissus and Goldmund	Herman Hesse	1102 4	12.50
Peter Camenzind	Herman Hesse	1168 7	9.95
The Prodigy	Herman Hesse	1174 1	9.95
The Hunting Gun	Yasushi Inoue	1213 6	7.95
Asylum Piece	Anna Kavan	1123 7	9.95
The Parson	Anna Kavan	1140 7	8.50
Sleep Has His House	Anna Kavan	1129 6	9.95
Who Are You?	Anna Kavan	1150 4	8.95
The Lady and the Little Fox Fur	Violette Leduc	1217 9	8.95
Confessions of a Mask	Yukio Mishima	1031 1	11.95
Children of the Albatross	Anaïs Nin	1165 2	9.95
Collages	Anaïs Nin	1145 8	9.95
The Four-Chambered Heart	Anaïs Nin	1155 5	9.95
Ladders to Fire	Anaïs Nin	1162 8	9.95
The Last Summer	Boris Pasternak	1099 0	8.50
The Devil in the Hills	Cesare Pavese	1118 0	9.95
The Moon and the Bonfire	Cesare Pavese	1119 9	9.95
Among Women Only	Cesare Pavese	1214 4	9.95
A Book of Nonsense	Mervyn Peake	1163 6	7.95
My Life	Edith Piaf	1111 3	9.95
The Spirit of Romance	Ezra Pound	1215 2	10.95
Pleasures and Regrets	Marcel Proust	1110 5	9.95
Flight Without End	Joseph Roth	1068 0	9.95
The Silent Prophet	Joseph Roth	1135 0	9.95
Weights and Measures	Joseph Roth	1136 9	9.95
Alberta and Jacob	Cora Sandel	1184 9	9.95
Essays in Aesthetics	Jean-Paul Sartre	1209 8	9.95
The Three-Cornered World	Natsume Soseki	1156 3	9.95
Paris France	Gertrude Stein	1197 0	9.95
Midnight Tales	Bram Stoker	1134 2	9.95
The Birds	Tarjei Vesaas	1143 1	9.95
The Ice Palace	Tarjei Vesaas	1189 X	9.95
Spring Night	Tarjei Vesaas	1122 9	9.95
The Boat in the Evening	Tarjei Vesaas	1198 9	9.95
The Redemption of Elsdon Bird	Noel Virtue	1166 0	9.95